Kama Kahani

Mistress to the Yuvraj

Kama Kahani

Mistress to the Yuvraj

Sanyogita Rathore

EBURY PRESS

An imprint of Penguin Random House

EBURY PRESS

USA | Canada | UK | Ireland | Australia
New Zealand | India | South Africa | China

Ebury Press is part of the Penguin Random House group of companies
whose addresses can be found at global.penguinrandomhouse.com

Published by Penguin Random House India Pvt. Ltd
4th Floor, Capital Tower 1, MG Road,
Gurugram 122 002, Haryana, India

Penguin
Random House
India

First published by Random House India 2009
This edition published in Ebury Press by Penguin Random House India 2020

10 9 8 7 6 5 4 3 2

ISBN 9788184000238

Typeset in Sabon by Inosoft Systems, Noida

www.penguin.co.in

For Rajni, my best friend and editor

CHAPTER ONE

YUVRAJ SHIVENDRA SINGH SHEKHAWAT, heir to the princely state of Jaigarh, stood just inside the main durbar hall's silver doors, glowering handsomely. He was tall, dark, and arrestingly good looking; some would say cruelly so—his face was so accustomed to its mocking, arrogant cast. He had spent the last few weeks on the fringes of the North West Frontier, battling nomadic tribes, and felt incongruous in his usual surroundings. It was strange, he thought, to have sparred in war just a few days ago and to now have to pretend to be part of the lavish festivities of the best of Rajput society again. He chose the word 'pretend' deliberately; the yuvraj never quite fit in, in polite society. There had to be more to life, he thought.

But the crowded haveli did look resplendent, with its dazzling gold tissue curtains and velvet gold facings. Dhruv Singh Pauota, a chief in his army, was getting married to the only daughter of the zamindar of Marsuda—an alliance that had been plotted by the family elders. Rumour had it that the bride was pockmarked and stout, though as nobody except the groom's mother had seen her, it was yet to be confirmed. Not that it would make any difference; the bride's dowry would take care of wagging tongues—it was not every day that a thousand camels and three hundred acres of land exchanged hands.

Countless twinkling diyas, generously sprinkled like rice over the vast floor, cast a brilliant daze over the canopied courtyard. There, the dancers whirled to the beat of the ghumar, whirling east and then west in a continuous, hypnotic rhythm. Celebrating the first event of the auspicious season, common women dressed in their most lustrous, embroidered, silk poshaaks, and men in majestic jodhpurs offset with flaming ruby buttons adorned the hall below. Young girls, dressed in the colours of the rainbow, showed off poshaaks in the brightest shades of green, canary yellow veils, scarlet lehengas glittering with crystals, and gold tassels braided through their long, flowing tresses. The nubile nautch girls in their swirling chiffon lehengas moved about the dance floor in graceful circles, while the ladies of noble birth, dressed in their richer yet more understated poshaaks, sat high up on the first floor, veiled by a latticed wall delicate enough for the men to see the bevy of young girls through it, yet elaborate enough for the women to be obscured behind it. This wall was usually powerful provocation for virile young Rajput men.

Shivendra, however, had other thoughts on his mind; he had decided to suffer the festive celebrations for a few hours before slipping out for a rendezvous with his sensuous mistress, Ayesha Begum. He had first met her at a feast given at his hunting lodge a few months ago, and she had caught his fancy for the next two weeks. He was ready to move on now; he had a very low threshold for boredom. Shivendra was preceded by his reputation for new conquests, whether they lay in the battlefield or in the bedrooms of glittering havelis. Indeed, his past had been the subject of many hushed whispers and gossip sessions in Jaigarh.

Unknown to Jaigarh society, though, Shivendra had only ever turned his irresistible charms on willing women who could equal him in experience, never having to work at the peak of his powers. However, the marriage proposals were steadily increasing every day; he was considered to be the most eligible bachelor in Rajasthan. Yes, even the young prince's scandalous past, overflowing with tales of debauchery and indiscretions, was not enough to put women off.

Shivendra's arresting features wore a nonchalant, slightly bored expression as he glanced around, looking up at a covey of eager young girls standing directly atop, herded behind the latticed separation and gazing at him in breathless anticipation. He couldn't have looked more aloof.

And then he saw her.

His restless gaze settled on a bewitchingly beautiful girl, not older than seventeen. She was angelically exquisite, from her radiant honey-coloured skin to her dark eyes, rimmed with kohl and speaking a language all their own. His experienced eye skimmed the layers of brocade and chiffon, noting with satisfaction that her form was irrefutably feminine, in fact, most luscious. Not only was she undeniably sensuous, her carriage was strikingly aristocratic. Her flawless, oval face and elegant neck were tilted at an imperial angle; long black hair was braided carelessly and threaded with gold and jewels, lustrous in the light of hundreds of diyas; her eyes, large and lovely, smote him from afar.

Shivendra stood spellbound, unable to tear his eyes away from the young woman; never in his wildest dreams—and of these there had been many—had he envisioned anything like her. Upon a closer look, she looked engrossed herself, only, her undivided attention was fixed on the flaming dancers; the twinkle in her eyes betrayed her enthusiasm.

Nandini wanted to dance with the nautch girls swirling around in the central courtyard below. Her feet, hidden beneath yards of rose pink brocade, were already tapping to the exhilarating beat of the drums.

Below her, the durbar hall packed in a considerable crowd. The delayed hour did nothing to thin the crush, only making the crowd more boisterous and wanton with each passing hour. Gold-rimmed crystal glasses were drained of alcohol almost as soon as they were served, while the guests gorged on ample quantities of delicacies: trays laden with roganjosh, kebabs, succulent chicken tikkas, and tables full of sweetmeats.

Nandini, who had arrived a few weeks ago from Multan to spend some time with her bua, her father's sister, and her cousin Devika, was awestruck to see such grandeur. She had been single-handedly raised by her father who had felt it more important to familiarize her with ancient texts of Sanskrit, history lessons of their ancestors, and mythological tales of chivalry and bravery, rather than have her spend time with her dai, who coached her in the fine art of cooking and being the perfect housewife. Her father was an intelligent man, often spending days locked up in his room reading books, but he was inept at administering their estate. Their home had fallen into a hopeless state of disrepair, the land refused to yield anything except for a few worthless shrubs, and the place had gradually deteriorated, slowly eating up her dowry and their other properties scattered around Peshawar. Her aunt had offered to take care of Nandini temporarily, and had assured her father he would see his daughter's wedding that very year. A sudden increase in rhythm broke into Nandini's thoughts. She took it all in, wanting to join the dancers. She twitched excitedly, but not only on this count. Beneath all the fun and frivolity, the flirting and dialogue, she was subconsciously aware of being the focus of someone's watchful gaze.

Peeping over the corner of the latticed wall, she caught only the shadow of a striking, majestic man before the colourful, swirling movement of the nautch girls removed him from her sight again. With her heart in her mouth, she stood there transfixed, impatient and anxious for another look at this enigmatic stranger. The dancers moved in her favour again, and the man was laid bare to her; their eyes met and stayed fixed on each other, for what seemed like an eternity.

Handsome was too insipid a word to describe him; he was magnificent and captivating, with glossy black hair and features that looked like they were carved out of stone. Masculine and powerfully built, his physique rivalled his aristocratic looks. His immaculately styled midnight blue sherwani fit his broad shoulders perfectly, the sapphire buttons gleaming like his raven eyes. Eyes that were still looking at her, eyes whose gaze Nandini suddenly found herself trembling under. Annoyingly, she saw that there was no evidence of any conflict in the man's eyes, just the confidence of knowing the turmoil they caused.

Snapping out of her reverie, she heard just then snatches of a hushed conversation between the women beside her, as they gossiped about the imposing figure standing below.

'Look, there the handsome devil is! He is looking at me, I always knew the yuvraj was interested, ever since he kissed me at Ragini's wedding,' gushed the first woman.

The yuvraj, Nandini realized, with a jolt. And obviously, he had attracted more than just her attention that night.

'You mean you kissed him. Anyway, that hardly counts since he kissed half the women at the naatch that day. Except me,' the second voice complained peevishly.

The first woman laughed. 'You are just fretful because he ignored your advances that day. Come on, we both know it, if the handsome yuvraj were to summon you, you would kiss the ground his feet walked on.'

'Yes I would, like any other warm-blooded woman. He is rumoured to be richer than Shahenshah Akbar, and as we can all see, devastatingly handsome. I wish...'

Nandini's attention shifted back to the man she now knew to be the notoriously famous yuvraj. His raw, sensuous energy and wicked, dark looks, each movement dictating notice, warned her away; every instinct for self-preservation admonished her to stay away from the yuvraj. Leopards, after all, can never change their spots, she recalled the advice of women who had spoken of him. His scandalous conquests amongst the beau monde couldn't possibly be exaggerated, yet it was impossible to ignore his inescapable magnetism.

Nandini wrapped her heavily embroidered brocade odhna tightly around herself, in spite of the warmth of thousands of bodies crowded into the hall and the infinite diyas glittering around her. Her rose pink-and-gold silk ensemble complemented the rubies adorning her ears, generously lent to her by her aunt. She felt horribly out of date—having just arrived from Lahore, she had no fineries styled in the latest fashions of these parts.

'Nandini, how many times have I told you to remain veiled in public? This is not Lahore that you may do as you please. Now hurry, my child, before an evil eye settles on you, pull your veil down.' Nandini's paternal aunt, Shreyas Kanwar, hurriedly pulled the chiffon drape over Nandini's face, so she finally lost eye contact with the yuvraj. Majestically, the lady dragged her niece and daughter Devika, who had arrived next to Nandini after scouring the masses below, to the end of the adjacent corridor.

'Now tell me, both of you. Did you fancy any young man today?' she enquired eagerly. 'Don't be shy. You know I'm not like the usual conservative mothers. Just tell me who you like and I can send them formal proposals. All of them are rich and well connected, so there is no chance of your having picked an impoverished zamindar,' she said, beaming.

'Ma hukum, there is nobody even close to decent here,' Devika ventured.

'Rubbish, darling. There are so many eligible men in the room, like...like Kripal Singh.'

'The one with a stone eye?' Devika asked with a teasing smile.

'What about Surya Singh?'

'He has six illegitimate children from his previous mistresses and they are all living with him,' Devika offered.

'Maan Suryavanshi then?'

'He never ceases to stare at the mirror—rumour has it that he has mirror walls installed in his private chambers, and I shudder to imagine his bathing area.'

'Rajkumar Lavesh Singh?' she ventured desperately.

'Drinks like a fish and last heard, had lost his village estate in a game of dice,' Devika whispered to her much amused cousin. Her mother shook her head, unamused.

'You girls are so fussy these days. In my time we had no such choices. My mother married me off to your father at fourteen and I was sixteen when I saw his face for the first time,' Shreyas Kanwar grumbled, leaving to join a group of matchmaking mothers at the far end of the room. The girls returned to their earlier positions.

'Nandini, stay away from him. Men like him eat women like you for breakfast' Devika gave her a cousin a knowing glance, having seen the exchange between Nandini and the predatorial yuvraj take place. Nandini eyed her cousin from behind her cumbersome veil, her eyes involuntarily moving back to the yuvraj's towering form.

'Do you know who he is?' Nandini asked as Devika turned away, intending to join her mother. 'Someone important, I presume?' she mumbled, to no one in particular. She knew he was the yuvraj, but was uncertain of his lineage; she had little knowledge of such things.

'More on the lines of the most important person in Jaigarh,' her cousin told her. 'He is Shivendra Singh, son of the Maharaja and Maharani of Jaigarh, and heir apparent to Jaigarh and Kunihar in Himachal Pradesh.' She explained that the yuvraj's mother, an only child, belonged to the princely state of Kunihar, and in time, Shivendra would inherit Kunihar as well as Jaigarh because he was the only male heir in line to the accession of Kunihar, bestowing him with unentailed property and fortune besides doubling his military strength.

'What else?' Nandini asked, restlessly fidgeting with the edge of her odhna. Stories of his fame and fortune were not what she wanted to hear. What of his heart, she wondered.

'One of the officers talking to him—the tall one on his right—is Manvendra, his right-hand man,' Devika explained. 'Shivendra is also the most coveted catch in the marriage market—apparently the Maharaja of Mewar is very keen to have him as a son-in-law. I expect a formal proclamation will probably be announced shortly, but you know how rumours are. And you, you'd better keep your distance, Nandini, that is, if you don't want to be chewed up and spat out.' She winked at her cousin and grinned.

Nandini laughed, recollecting the gossip she had heard of this legendary lothario. 'So this is *the* Shivendra Singh. For all you know they are all ridiculous rumours—after all, nothing seems to be more expeditious to assassinate character than fabrication. Anyway,' she shrugged carelessly, 'I am not planning to have an affair, an audience with him would more than suffice.' The nagging voice in her head admonished her for lying, but she hurriedly brushed it away.

'The Yuvraj of Jaigarh is not someone you could have an "audience" with, at least not if you are standing up,' Devika said wickedly, her eyes twinkling. She added, 'He is supposed to have fought and won over the Pashtun tribe all by himself, and then benevolently bestowed back their lives and land. Most soldiers would take pleasure in parading the blackened faces of their foes in the alleys of the bazaar, some even torturing the vanquished men with sword and shot.'

'Ragini was telling me he is sleeping with Ayesha Begum, the most famous courtesan from Lakhnau,' Devika continued. 'With her...talent and ah, other attributes, he hardly needs to look around for female company.'

Nandini's eyes lingered, returning to their earlier perusal, studying the hawkish features of the yuvraj's ruthlessly handsome face from behind the latticed wall. Irrespective of what rumour said, her instincts told her otherwise; surely, there was more to this man than these tales.

Suddenly, she felt Shivendra's intense gaze piercing into her again. It was like being stood out in the sun in the middle of the palace courtyard, for all to see, so keen was his scrutiny.

The blood rushed up to her face, the heat staining her cheeks a fierce shade of crimson. Impulsively, she refused to lower her eyes—after all she had caught him staring first. She rearranged her face to resemble a cold mask and glared back at him, daring him to look away first. And he did succumb—but why did she feel like he was still winning? For Shivendra's eyes had moved lower, eyeing her breasts, which strained the thin silk of her blouse, with pure, lustful, male appreciation, then her narrow waist, down to her shapely legs, revealed in outline by the clinging brocade of her lehenga. The corners of his mouth turned up slightly as Nandini was finally forced to lower her eyes demurely. She decided instead to fix her eyes on the polished mosaic marble floor.

This time, Devika wasn't the only one to notice the exchange.

'Looks like someone did catch your fancy,' remarked Manvendra, Shivendra's second-in-command and closest friend. 'Has the lion met his match finally?' he joked, following the direction of his friend's fixed stare.

'I need something to relieve the boredom, Manvendra,' Shivendra said, casually ignoring the question. 'Pretty little thing. I need someone willing to acquaint me with her.'

'She is of noble birth, not one of the nautch girls that you can get "acquainted" with,' Manvendra pointed out, consciously aware of the divisions between the zenana, the women's section, usually restricted to the upper balconies and corridors encased with latticed walls, and the mardana, the men's section in the main hall and courtyard.

'I want her.' It was a statement, not a demand. Shivendra, who was not accustomed to being refused anything, decided to take matters into his own hands. 'I am going to go up to her and introduce myself since there is nobody willing to arrange an encounter between us.'

Shivendra was already advancing through the congested hall, cutting across the courtyard to the winding staircase leading up to the zenana, in the direction of the mystery girl, when Manvendra caught up with him.

'All right, listen to me! I will arrange for you to be introduced to her tomorrow, but not here. We will cause a scandal if we go up to the zenana,' he said breathlessly.

Shivendra eyed his childhood friend resentfully. 'Concealing things from me?' A sudden feeling of irrational jealousy took him by surprise. 'Why didn't you tell me you are well acquainted with her?'

'Because I am not,' he said, smiling. 'I have had the pleasure of meeting her cousin once. Her mother is keen to see us married,' Manvendra said. 'She almost threw her daughter at me at Pandit Ravikishen's sitar recital. You had an...ah...prior commitment and did not attend, as I recall,' he said, knowing better that to take Ayesha Jaan's name in front of him, especially at a time like this.

'Prior commitment? Oh yes, in any case, suffering Pandit Ravikishen's music for an entire evening would have definitely ensured at least a headache,' Shivendra said dismissively, then bit his tongue against further criticism of his mother's beloved musician. 'What else do you know about the girl? I have never seen her in Jaigarh before.'

'Only that her name is Nandini, she is the daughter of a penniless zamindar in Lahore, and recently moved to Jaigarh to live with her aunt.'

A woman with neither dowry nor family—he knew how to handle her. He would lavish her with extravagant presents and opulent jewellery. It just made it easier for what he had in mind. He had no intention of marrying her, even if she was the most gorgeous woman his eyes had ever settled upon. For what was beauty for but to entertain himself, to spend a few moments of pleasure with her before they both had to move on?

CHAPTER TWO

THE MAHARANI OF JAIGARH sat on a plush silk divan in the lavish quarters of the zenana, listening to her maid Kaushalya as she filled her in on the scandals of the season. She sighed as the woman massaged her feet with warm mustard oil—their age-old ritual. Kaushalya was a treasure trove of gossip, famous for knowing rumours before they had officially become rumours. Two maids, hidden from view, fanned two huge, heavy satin fans embroidered with silver across the length of the verandas, spreading the warm afternoon breeze out to every corner together with the intoxicating fragrance of the sweet roses and flame of the forest flowers that laced the garden walls. The palatial zenana was a series of opulent chambers interlinked with latticed corridors that opened out into several confined gardens. It was spring and even in the arid climate of Rajputana, the garden was at its zenith, the kaleidoscopic bands of blossoming flowers in the intensely hued and abundant green lawns complemented by streams of water delicately overflowing from the marble fountains. The setting sun cast a champagne hue on all of it, soaking the scene in a soft light as the maharani reached out to pour herself another cup of warm almond milk.

'I heard the maharaja is arranging an alliance between Mewar's princess, Bhanupriya, and Shivendra? Is it serious?' Kaushalya paused, pouring more oil into her palm from the ornate brass bottle that was placed on the cool marble floor.

The maharani took her time before answering, not entirely sure of her husband's intentions. 'Of course not, Kaushalya, but the maharaja is keen Shivendra settles down soon so he is blessed with a son. Left to his own devices, he will never marry.'

'Our prince will never lack for proposals, even without his title and money, women would be flocking to him like bees to honey, in spite of his ah...colourful ways,' Kaushalya said indulgently, her tone honeyed. 'But,' she hurried on, 'I hear Bhanupriya is not worthy of our prince—my sister's daughter-in-law is her masseuse, and she complains the girl is spoilt and throws tantrums that are reputed to wake up the dead and...' she whispered conspiratorially, 'the princess drinks herself to sleep every night—says she can't afford to waste water in a desert and quenches her thirst with canisters of alcohol.'

'Are you absolutely sure, Kaushalya?' the maharani asked sternly.

'I swear on my grandchildren, Hukum. If you wish, I will ask the daughter-in-law to come to the palace and tell you all that she knows,' Kaushalya said, folding her hands reverently.

'What a mismatch! My son would stray even

more if he were tied to someone so wayward, the maharani exclaimed. 'My only wish is for my son to be happy, as for this proposal, the maharaja might appear a little...forceful, but eventually, it will be left to Shivendra completely.

'Maharani sa, I hope you are not being overly indulgent. I fear the yuvraj will pick up someone from the street,' Kaushalya said, wrinkling her brow in mock concern.

'I only want him to be happy, and if his happiness lies with a woman of low birth, I will support it,' the maharani said flatly but firmly.

'Of course, but,' Kaushalya said tartly, tongue in cheek, 'the maharaja might not.'

'That's enough, Kaushalya,' the maharani warned indignantly.

'Kaushalya dai has taken to gossiping about my alleged affairs, I gather.' From the arched hallway, the prince's low, careless voice reached them, just before Shivendra walked on to the veranda, the stark white of his angrakha offset by the fiery orange of his safa, a velvet-encased sword held casually in his hand. The mischievous gleam in his eye gave nothing away as he bent down to touch his mother's and then his daai's feet respectfully, before settling down on the divan by his mother's side. 'My marriage is my own affair, Dai, don't worry my mother with tales of my alleged escapades,' he said, glancing at Kaushalya.

Shivendra turned around to hug his mother affectionately, enveloping her in a bear hug. Kaushalya resumed massaging the maharani's feet, smiling fondly at this display of affection before declaring, 'Don't use that arrogant tone with me, Yuvraj,' she mocked, 'I have seen you crawling around in your nappies. You know there is no one closer to my heart, my heart brims with nothing but love for you, my dearest.' The yuvraj smiled at her charmingly. 'And I won't give you reason to let that change, Kaushalya dai.'

'Then make this old woman happy and get married,' Kaushalya remarked, seizing the chance. 'The town is abuzz with rumours of you and your latest woman, its time you bound yourself down with a respectable woman.'

'I would make a wayward husband, Dai. The drudgery of domesticity holds no charms for me, and I have no intentions of being bound by some unfortunate girl…' He was interrupted when the door opened; his father entered the veranda, striding in stiffly.

The maharaja had just returned after surveying his estates. He was dressed in a cream angrakha kurta, lined with gold velvet. 'And what has my son done now?' He only looked into the maharani's lit-up eyes when Kaushalya scurried away, eyes on the ground and hands folded, out of respect.

The maharaja walked to the edge of the veranda and stood there, admiring the sweep of the abundant, luscious lawns, the air heavy with the incense of sweet-smelling blossoms. His imposing frame was silhouetted by the blaze of the descending sun.

'How are the farmers? How was your trip?' The maharani stood up, hurriedly changing the topic, hoping her husband hadn't heard Kaushalya's gibberish.

'Good,' he said, leaving her to decipher what she could from the monosyllabic answer. 'And you,' he said, turning around to face his son, 'will make more than just an old woman happy by settling down.' He remarked distantly, 'Shivendra, the kingdom needs an heir. I assume you have reached a decision regarding Princess Bhanupriya. We have patiently waited for you to fall in love but now in your thirty-first year, our...my patience is wearing thin.' Shivendra met the maharaja's glare defiantly as he carried on.

'I have heard rumours of another nautch girl, some Ayesha Begum,' is it? I have no intentions of invading your "privacy", he said, as he walked nonchalantly to the centre of the marbled floor, stopping just below the bejewelled chandelier, 'but it is high time you settled down into marital bliss with a woman of high birth and suitable upbringing.' The maharaja lifted his eyebrows as if inviting the yuvraj to challenge him.

Shivendra had been avoiding his father's speech by looking everywhere but at his face. Now that he was expected to say something, he matched his father's stare, before replying in the determined voice of somebody who had long since made up his mind. 'I will not marry Princess Bhanupriya, Dada.'

The maharaja ignored the yuvraj's words, instead choosing to concentrate on inspecting the rich ruby velvet of his sword case. 'Then marry someone else, there are several alliances you could choose from.'

Shivendra replied calmly, yet firmly, with just the slightest clench of his teeth. 'You seem to have misinterpreted what I said. I do not wish to marry any woman right now, princess or pauper, and I will definitely not do so under anyone's persuasion or initiation.'

'Shivendra, many times we need to find a balance between what we want to do and what we have to do. It is your duty towards your people and kingdom to marry. You have been linked with several young women over the last decade, but none of your relationships have reached the sacred fire. If you have someone in mind, I will ecstatically bless the union, but if that is not the case, you must consider marrying the Princess of Mewar.'

Shivendra remarked in a frosty tone, his features a determined mask of perseverance, 'I shall only marry when I meet a woman I want to marry, Dada.'

Inside the exquisitely frescoed domes of the queen's palace, the silence amplified menacingly as father and son stood face to face, neither lowering his gaze, their set jaws mirroring each other. The maharani hurriedly interrupted the argument before it became too heated. 'Perhaps we need to give our son some time to consider the proposal before he commits? You must respect Shivendra's decision. After all, we cannot force him to marry anyone.'

'Respect? If he respected me, he would do as I say and marry the Princess of Mewar,' the maharaja protested, with a beseeching glance to his wife.

The Maharani of Jaigarh held out a finely manicured hand to her son. 'Shivendra,' she said, 'darling, you have sown your...ah...escorted so many women without it leading to anything serious. I'm certain that even if the princess is not a perfect match for you, we could arrange a suitable alliance, we only ask for you to be willing.'

In her son's eyes there was a vacant look that tore at her heart. 'Is there someone else? Whoever she is, I will ensure you marry her, even if she is of low birth or a pauper.' There was an implicit appeal in her eyes as she waited for him to answer her.

'Very well.' Shivendra's voice was cold and expressionless. 'If I don't find love by the end of this year, I will happily marry anybody you choose.'

'Well, then,' the maharaja said spiritedly, all evidence of the turbulent argument having evaporated faster than the drops of rain from the surface of the desert. 'You have made me proud, my son. The fiefdom, estates, the people need an heir, a son to carry on this legacy. The princess would make a fine queen, but we will happily accept anybody else that you may fall in love with...the chances of which are bleak to none.' He beamed at his son, and then turning to his wife, 'You had better get on with the marriage preparations, invitations to be issued, artisans to be commissioned with a wardrobe fit enough for my only son.'

'Yes, yes, I am delighted. You don't have to marry the princess, my dearest, I am sure you will find love,' the maharani said with a reassuring smile. 'I shall get a different set of buttons made in gold and diamonds for every outfit of yours...The world will see what a glorious affair it will be.' But Shivendra was not listening, he was on his way to ride back to his haveli. He waited by the main palace entrance for his horseman to fetch his marwar from the royal stables. He had glimpsed Princess Bhanupriya last year at the archery competition where she had arrived with her father, but try as he might, he could not find it in himself to think of her as his bride-to-possibly-be. He closed his eyes and desperately tried directing all his energies towards concentrating on an image of the Princess of Mewar; but his mind was suddenly invaded with images of the sensuous Nandini, that luscious, full mouth begging to be kissed, the doe-like eyes so potently seductive, her voluptuous feminine form which made him almost ache to touch her. His body hardened at the thought of her calling his name out aloud with pleasure. She would rake her nails against his weather-roughened back, begging him not to stop, he vowed, just like many a woman had done before.

He could still recall her eyes, blazing with intelligence, twinkling with wordless invitation; her flawless ivory skin, tinted with gold by the fiery Rajputana sun. Nandini from Lahore...he would have to find out more about her.

Yes Nandini, so full of fire, far spicier than the famous red chillies of the Thar. Princess Bhanupriya, on the other hand, was insipid, bland, tasteless; he couldn't even envision her form for a minute. Marriage to her would be torture. But forget marriage, he had a year to think of that. For now, his mind had no place for anyone but Nandini, and after her, there would be someone else. He would just have to settle with one of them, the one who was most suitable and whose match was most advantageous for his father, and learn to live with a woman he didn't love or desire. This might be better—his friends spoke of the danger of all-consuming attractions; at least such a woman wouldn't fill every breath he took with her presence; her images wouldn't creep into his mind without warning, invading him when he least expected them.

His handsome marwar trotted into sight, led faithfully by the bowing horseman. Shivendra mounted the horse and galloped towards the iron gates, winding his way through the mango and neem trees. Riding into his section of the palace, Shivendra looked back at his mother's palace.

Seducing the mysterious Nandini was of paramount importance, everything else could wait. He would have her, that much was certain.

Two hours later, a horseman had been dispatched to Nandini's house, with a letter safely tucked in the breast pocket of his angrakha.

'Nandiniiiiii, Nandiniiiiiiiiiiiiii!'

The maid, who was busy smearing the soles of Nandini's alabaster feet with a paste of saffron and sandalwood soaked overnight in rose water, was startled enough by the loud cries to smudge the saffron fluid all the way up to her charge's calves. Having recently been employed in the household, she was still not used to Devika, who screeched like a common fisherwoman at any hint of activity. Indeed, the household was surprised the stained glass windows were still intact. And Nandini was doing her own bit to threaten them. 'Coming, Devika! I'm coming!' she screamed, possibly louder than her cousin, who pranced in the courtyard below. Nandini hitched up the hem of her lehenga and ran down the length of the corridor, staining the sandstone with red footprints. She hurried down the stairs, her mango yellow odhna tangling with the chamelis in the brass flower pots by the veranda. A slip and a swerve later, she veered to a halt just before her cousin. 'What happened? Are you all right?' she asked, still catching her breath.

Before she could reply, a well-dressed horseman approached her with a note in hand. 'Hukum, this just arrived for you.' With a bow, the servant retreated back a step. 'I have strict instructions by the palace servant to give this letter only to you.'

The cousins exchanged looks.

Devika snatched the letter from his hand, scandalizing the poor man with her unladylike behaviour. To their amusement, he was fast colouring into an unflattering shade of beet red. 'A letter addressed to you,' she said, tongue in cheek.

What Nandini wanted to say was, 'Give it to me right now'.

Instead what she did say was, 'Really? I don't think it can be for me, I hardly know anyone here.' And with that, she casually perched her bottom on the silk divan.

Devika stood there, smiling like a cat. 'It is stamped with the yuvraj's royal seal,' she said, slowly and deliberately.

Nandini widened her pink pout and picked up a piece of cashew barfi. 'Why on earth would the yuvraj be writing to me? she asked. He must have the names mixed up.'

Devika shrugged her delicate shoulders carelessly. 'I guess I will just have to find out, fetch me the paper cutter please.' Two could play at a game.

Nandini promptly sank another two feet into the cushions, listening to Devika go on. 'It must be about the Kunihar wedding—the yuvraj's cousin is going to be married soon and Shivendra is probably feeling the pressure to get married as well. You know, I think he fancies me, why else would he be writing to me? I was wearing my green lehenga at the wedding; Mother tells me I look like a heavenly apsara when I wear green, though I have always known no man could resist my charms...only I wasn't trying to charm the yuvraj. Maybe he was so blinded by my beauty that he just can't help himself, poor thing!'

Devika ripped open the note. A wicked smile crossed her face, and Nandini had to force herself not to steal a peek. When she looked up to meet her cousin's eye, her face had been painstakingly rearranged into appearing detached and indifferent. 'Let me guess. Is it bad news?'

'Depends on what you call bad news. It is Shivendra,' she announced dramatically. She crumpled the note in her hand. 'If you will excuse me, I must take my leave now, I have...ummm,' she cleared her throat, 'a prior commitment to attend to,' she said, eyebrows raised. With a flounce of her muslin lehenga, she turned towards the staircase. Nandini's distress was immediate and apparent, washing over her features like the first monsoon shower that came without warning.

'Oh, I forgot, I promised to pickle the mangoes for Ma today. I guess I will just meet the yuvraj some other time,' Devika said with mock indifference.

Nandini tried to shape her lips into some semblance of a smile, then had to abort the intention. 'Uhh, he might be disappointed, what if he was waiting for us?'

'Hmm, that's just too bad. Anyway you just said you don't want to meet him.' Devika casually knotted her waist-length curls into a loose knot at her nape, half walking out of the arched doorway.

'Devika, wait. Let's go for a while, just to have a look.'

Devika stopped, turned around slowly, and stood there pondering; her face wore a serious look. 'Nandini, don't build castles in the air,' she admonished her cousin. 'Shivendra is a womanizer and we both know a leopard can't change its spots. The letter might be for you but I would warn you not to speak with him.'

'So why shouldn't I be talking to him? He seems nice.' Nandini half sulked, half asked.

'Nice? I don't think Shivendra can be described as "nice", no—anything but that,' Devika warned, with a wave of her hand. 'Anyway under most circumstances, unmarried girls do not talk to men alone. Ma will throw a fit if she knew—though she would gladly make an exception if the boy is as eligible,' she added with a wry smile.

'If he is so infamous, why is he considered so eligible?' Nandini challenged.

'You don't understand.' Devika hesitated. 'Involving yourself with Shivendra is like playing with fire and when you play with fire, you often get burnt.'

'Often, but not always. I am willing to risk it.' Nandini stood her ground, all pretext of not caring having vaporized into thin air. 'Is he a criminal?' she demanded, with a stubborn tilt of her chin.

'No, not at all, more like the protector of our lands,' Devika said, annoyed with her cousin for not being able to see the obvious.

'A gold digger?' she asked and then added hurriedly, 'I have none so he will be disappointed.'

'Nandini, Shivendra has enough wealth to buy Rajputana five times over if he chooses to do so,' Devika said, sounding like her Sanskrit teacher explaining Vedic verses to his inattentive pupils. 'But please trust me when I tell you that you must stay away. Don't let any bond form or strengthen, because when these ties snap—which sooner or later they will—you will be left nursing a very broken heart. One that might still mend with time, but the remnants of your reputation—those you will never be able to piece back together.'

'You sound like someone's mother, Devika!' Nandini admonished. 'I really don't care for my reputation as you put it,' she said defiantly, 'and I am not going to get my heart broken by him. I just want to meet him once. I cannot understand why he has this effect on me. I have never reacted in such a ridiculous manner before, and I desire neither his pedigree nor his privilege or prosperity. And I just want to take a chance, do something out of the ordinary—we never do, you know.' This last statement was open to debate of course; Nandini had hardly been known to conform, back in Lahore. Her restraints here were beginning to chafe, however.

Devika spent the next few minutes explaining that she couldn't fathom why Nandini was responding to a complete stranger in such a brazen, wanton fashion. Why, she had hardly met him, and if one look from him was enough for her to abandon reason and blindly agree to a clandestine meeting, she feared for what would come next.

'You could always accompany me to the Rani ka Bagh,' Nandini said hopefully, at last.

'Rani ka Bagh? Surely you are not going there alone—it is completely isolated at this hour.'

'Fine, then I will just have to brave the dangers of the night alone.' Nandini looked dolefully at her cousin. 'There could be barbaric dacoits, wild animals, evil spirits, man-eating creepers...'

Devika rolled her eyes skyward. 'This is Jaigarh, not some lost land from your fantasies.' She gave her cousin a long peneterating look. 'We will only stay there for half an hour, okay?' Nandini flung herself at Devika and enveloped her in a bear hug. 'I still don't approve,' Devika said, squeezing out of the impossibly tight embrace. 'Anyway, I will get my shawl,' she said, walking towards her room to accompany her cousin.

'Devika,' Manvendra said, an uncertain smile on his face, 'what a surprise to see you here.'

'Not a very pleasant one though,' she said sweetly, a false smile plastered on her face, knowing very well the entire meeting had been orchestrated by the yuvraj.

'Yes, but none that you couldn't have avoided...if you had wanted to that is.' The implication of the veiled remark hung heavily in the air. Devika blushed, angry at the insinuation that she had actually 'wanted' to come here. Devika and Manvendra stood, at loggerheads, glaring at each other. Any longer and Nandini feared they would resort to a fist fight!

She hastily interrupted the conversation. 'Devika,' she pulled her cousin back, glancing nervously at the floor while pulling her veil lower, her eyes moving from her cousin to Shivendra, who was walking towards them, and back again. Manvendra recomposed himself, addressing Devika again, 'I heard your sister has come to visit you from Lahore...and ah...this is Yuvraj Shivendra.'

Shivendra materialized next to his friend and nudged Manvendra with his elbow. His friend abruptly engaged Devika in a conversation, which, it was clear, she had no intention of being absorbed in.

Shivendra turned his attention to his conquest; she had come, as he had known she would. He tilted his head to the left and studied Nandini's profile from under hooded eyes: the impeccable, stately nose, that obstinate chin, those generous, luscious lips. She was even more captivating up close. He languidly dropped his gaze to admire her slim, delicate shoulders, before his eyes drifted down to the seductive curve of muslin-covered breasts, just barely visible through the chiffon odhna. The girl was voluptuous, he knew, though he couldn't tell much under the layers of muslin and chiffon. Quickly, he abandoned his appraisal, raising his eyes to meet hers directly.

But Nandini wasn't even looking at him. He was used to women throwing themselves at him, and had taken her ready compliance as further evidence that this was to be the case. This was going to be more of a challenge than he had anticipated.

'Let me show you around the garden,' he said, smiling politely, masking his annoyance. How dare she not look at him? But perhaps the young thing was shy; after all, she had just recently entered Jaigarh's high society.

Nandini inclined her face to look up at his handsome, tanned face. All her instincts told her to turn around and walk away, as fast as she could. She could feel his eyes caressing her, and a flood of excitement assaulted her senses, staining her cheeks crimson. Shivendra hadn't missed a beat, practised as he was, and he saw her absent-mindedly chew on her full bottom lip, before she nervously adjusted her odhna.

Her eyes darted around, still refusing to meet his. He could only imagine what had made her blush. She was definitely aware of him, but getting this sheltered young lovely to admit to this attraction was going to be another thing.

Yet, if anything, she looked prettier when she blushed, and the flushed ivory skin and heaving bosom were an indication of what might come next. He took a step forward, standing just behind her, the shadow of a smile lifting his lips.

'You have haunted me ever since I saw you at Dhruv Pauota's wedding celebrations,' he whispered, his chin brushing her ear.

Her shoulders stiffened. She was used to male contact, having been brought up with the village boys, but this felt different. It sent a chill down her spine.

Shivendra was aware of the effect he had on women, he was confident she was drawn to his charms and would react now, even if she refused to actually acknowledge his carnal appeal. 'It was not my intention to do so, especially not to someone so unknown,' she answered half distractedly, staring at the tips of her toes, which peeped out from under her lehenga. She knew he wouldn't believe this; after all she had returned his heated appraisal with her own.

Shivendra looked amused. He took her by the elbow and led her forward. 'I will just have to introduce myself to you and then we will no longer be strangers,' he said, smiling at her, 'Shivendra Singh'.

Nandini continued mauling her lower lip as she walked along the rows of lavender and cherry flowers, secretly taking in every detail of Shivendra. She would lock these away in her memory, the scene to be recalled and re-enacted when she lay alone in her bed at night, or on lazy afternoons when she could pretend to water the plants or pickle the raw mangoes and instead, daydream about the dashing yuvraj to her heart's content. She had heard of great love affairs, and perhaps this was the beginning of hers.

He had the darkest eyes, eyes that had the power to make her heart beat agitatedly. And his body, the kind of body young unmarried girls giggled about and married women ogled at with lust-filled eyes from behind their vibrant multicoloured veils. She secretly admired the fit of the tight churidar and fitted jodhpuri coat he wore.

Lost in her thoughts, Nandini tripped lightly on an overgrown root protruding from the ground. Shivendra reached out to steady her with his arm. Her full breasts came up against his white linen angrakha, a flagrant assault on his senses. She reached only till his shoulders, she saw, though she was above average height. He was that tall.

His hands moved down her back, moving further and further down until all at once, Nandini placed her palms flat on his broad chest. How dare he!

She tried to push him away gently, but her struggle only brought them closer, igniting her senses and sending sparks of passion darting through her body. Her breasts were still pressed against his chest and she could feel his own reaction to her, so close was his body to hers. He was, undeniably, the most magnificent man to have crossed her path, but that reputation of his preceded him and she couldn't afford to disregard that; her cousin was right.

Her heavy lids lowered, Nandini hid the expression in her eyes. 'If you would release me,' she said softly, not trusting her voice.

Shivendra didn't want to release her, she felt like she belonged right there, in his arms. She fit. But he knew he had to let her go. He unclasped his fingers, with intentional slowness, finally releasing the warm body that, for a few wonderful moments, had nestled against his.

Nandini took a half step back, the pink tinge on her cheeks deepening into a red as his fingers brushed the curve of her hip. Shivendra stepped closer, cornering her against the lotus pool. He wasn't giving up now.

Swiftly, he tilted her chin upwards, feeling her shiver beneath his touch. Immediately, he loosened his hold, his gaze transfixed by her full red lips, begging to be caressed. Carefully, he lowered his own mouth, careful not to break the spell, watching her eyes widen; the nervous swirl of her tongue on those slightly parted lips as his own covered them. Her mouth was wonderful against his—warm and wet and sweet. Unlike any other.

The press of his lips on her own shocked Nandini out of her unwitting reaction to the flirtatious yuvraj. Of course she had been kissed once before—a peck with one of the village boys in exchange for a mango when she was eleven—but that was nothing like the sensations that were aroused in her today. She was doing everything she had promised not to do in any case, but to be blatantly—not to forget enthusiastically—seduced in broad daylight? Maybe Devika was right; she was in danger of getting burnt, charred really. She swerved around, sliding from his arms, her heart pounding, her face burning, her entire being ablaze, on fire.

She glared at him. 'What are you doing?' she asked breathlessly.

'Come on, Nandini, must I teach you about love-making?' His voice was composed, giving no indication of the kiss having affected him at all. 'You wanted it as much as I did,' he said silkily.

'I have no intentions of refreshing my knowledge of lovemaking with you, Yuvraj. And I didn't try to kiss you, you did.'

'The eyes have a language of their own and yours were imploring to be kissed,' he said smoothly, eyes gleaming. 'You should know—ask yourself. I don't believe in wasting time, Nandini. We might as well admit what we want,' he continued, his voice low and determined. 'I want you to move into my palace with me; you will lack nothing.'

Nandini was scandalized. She had thought nothing could shock her. She opened her mouth, then closed it again; for once, words failed her completely. Her father would have given anything to see her dumbstruck, she thought, then shamed at the thought of what her father would say if he could see her now, propositioned by a prince like some woman of pleasure.

Flustered, she kept her face low, the veil obstructing his vision of her, and concentrated on examining the carpet of verdant lawns stretching below. What had she expected? A marriage proposal? An ardent declaration of eternal love? She was so naive.

Unaware of the conflict in Nandini's mind, Shivendra continued, 'You will have everything you can imagine—servants at your beck and call, rubies from Rangoon, emeralds from Colombia, silks from China, lehengas of the finest brocades woven with gold—though I would prefer you to wear none,' he said wickedly, not noticing her crestfallen face. 'We will travel to far-off exotic places; I will show you things you can never imagine exist—not in your wildest dreams, both inside and outside the sleeping chambers.'

Nandini abandoned all pretext of studying the grass as his last few words brought her back to the current situation. Her heart ached as if someone was piercing it with glass, and tears threatend to flow down her alabaster skin. She had never cried in public, and she wouldn't start now by showing this deplorable man how much he had hurt her. She bit down vehemently on her quivering lower lip, tasting blood, trying hard to concentrate on the more superficial pain this caused.

She concentrated on bringing a forced calm to her voice; then, she finally raised her face to meet his gaze evenly.

'I have neither the intention of, nor interest in, accepting any of your benevolent charity,' she said in the most level tone she could manage.

Shivendra was visibly taken back. He crossed his large forearms in front of his ample chest, waiting for her to finish.

Nandini put her hands on her hips, unconsciously mirroring the fury of her aunt when she screamed at the servants, trying her best to muster up courage she didn't think she had at the moment. 'I would rather walk out of your kingdom and Rajputana without a single silver coin in my hand, and sleep in the sand dunes with rattlesnakes before I even consider becoming your mistress!'

Shivendra threw back his head and laughed, a sinister, devilish laugh to Nandini's agitated mind.

His expressionless features were transformed into something more dissolute, the hooded eyes gleaming. Her cheeks were stained crimson as he lazily stripped her naked with his stare, an insulting smirk on his lips.

'You don't "wish" to be my mistress?'

She looked him dead in his eyes. 'Yes, Yuvraj Shivendra,' she said, emphasizing on the word. 'And now, if you will excuse me, I would prefer to go back to my life, to living with my aunt, without being bothered by you again.'

He stepped forward, covering her small form in his giant shadow. Nandini stood her ground, refusing to back away. 'I will decide your future and I want you to be my mistress!' he commanded.

Nandini couldn't understand what she was hearing. Men like Shivendra seemed to think they could have anybody—and yes, she acknowledged, they could. Men so majestic and entrancing that they attracted women like merchants to money. Not her though; the man she would marry must respect women; he would have to be a man who could boast of more than just an impressive pedigree or loads of gold stashed away in his treasury.

'I may not be of high birth, Yuvraj, but I would rather scrub floors than be a kept woman. My dignity is most valuable to me; I will not allow you to destroy me, and nothing—not your rubies or your piles of silks—is as precious as my...' her voice lessened to little more than a whisper, '...my self-respect.'

Shivendra had never been refused anything. How dare she, he found himself thinking again, only this time with an increased intensity. Something came over him. He had felt something with this woman; he knew she had felt it too, and desired him; he wouldn't let her forget this.

He pulled her towards him. 'I am the yuvraj of this kingdom, and everything—I repeat everything belongs to me—within the walls of this fort and in the deserts beyond. My word is authority, one that leaves you with no thought for your wants and wishes.' He raised his eyebrow imperiously. 'I am not asking you, I am telling you that if I desire you to be my paramour, you will do so without complaint... or choice.'

'Yuvraaj Shivendra, please let me go.' Nandini grappled against his hold, which further intensified his desire for her.

She struggled against him as he grasped her shoulders. Her breasts brushed against his manly chest, rising and falling swiftly with fear. Shivendra could feel desire stirring in him, and for the second time that day, he pressed his mouth to hers.

She resisted again, pushing him away, but he strove to awaken her to the passion he could tell was contained within her. These young virgins were easily stirred.

With one hand, he unclasped the tie that bound the lustrous locks of her hair, releasing them to caress his face with their silken touch. Wrapping his arms around her, bringing her disturbingly close to him, he pulled back her veil, jerking her face up and invading her mouth with kisses, his tongue expertly darting in to mate with hers in a blatant act of possession. Nandini, her body twining against his, had long ceased struggling, kissing him back with a passionate, unexpected ferocity.

It took all of his self-control to push her away. Every sense hungered for the fulfilment she promised, but he threw her from him. 'You didn't appear to be unwanting of my advances,' he said as calmly as he could, not a trace of turbulence in his voice though he was indescribably tormented. 'I could have taken you here and now. When you come to me, you will do so because you want it so badly that you will beg me to pleasure you, and when I finally take you to bed, you will not be thinking of self-respect.'

He looked at her flushed expression, the confused, rueful eyes, staring into his own. Nandini slipped past him, brushing against him lightly, retracing her steps past the fields of flowers. Shivendra's eyes never left her retreating figure, and as her steps slowed, with a twirl of her muslin lehenga, she turned to look back at him. Neither lowered their gaze; they were tied together by an invisible string which drew them to each other, a wordless attraction that required no language, even as they were divided by pride and what was certain to be censure from society.

Nandini's face hardened, at last. She was done with this seducer of women, never mind what attraction bound them together. With one last look, she turned and walked straight out of his line of vision.

Shivendra was left alone, staring at his reflection in the lotus pond. He had misjudged her. Then he straightened up. She drove a hard bargain—everything and everyone had a price, he just needed to find hers. It was only a matter of time.

CHAPTER THREE

'I AM SO DELIGHTED that you have finally come to stay with us, Nandini,' her aunt said, not bothering to look up from the intricate design she was knitting on a piece of silk. 'The haveli is much too large, massive actually, with its hundred and forty-two rooms, twelve durbar halls, and six courtyards. I know you are not used to such an extravagant lifestyle, but you will get used to it, dear. You will lack for no comfort. I have already lost count of the number of servants we have here—all trained to be as silent as fish swimming in the sea. I am so kind-hearted, I just can't refuse helping these villagers. It takes a lot to be...'

Devika, who was sitting beside Nandini, was suddenly struck by a coughing fit, appearing to have choked on her pickle and crisp tandoori bread. She was immediately silenced by the piercing glare her mother shot at her.

'As I was saying, it takes a lot to be as philanthropic as I have been. I am almost convinced I have been sent to this earth to serve others, like...Meerabai...no not her, she was married to both Girdhar Gopala (Lord Krishna) and the Rana Kumbha of Chittorgarh. It is sacrilege for me to think of a man other than my husband, you know how sati-savitri I am, placing my husband before God. Your uncle just doesn't realize how lucky he is to have been blessed with a wife such as me. When I was young, men used to queue up to get a glimpse of me. Even the Maharana of Hastinapur, he insisted he would marry me or die heirless, but his scheming mother rejected the proposal.

'There were rumours she did jadoo-tona on her son. Men are spineless creatures, never to be trusted. They are like banana peels, slippery and hollow. But as I was saying...oh, you girls distract me so much...I was sent to Earth to serve humanity, like the Buddha...yes, I feel I am a female version of the enlightened one; after all he did say something about generosity in the uh...what is that word? Gora memsahibs use it. Arre...yes, trifle pudding?'

'You mean the triple truth. Buddha said a generous heart, kind speech, and a life of service and compassion are the things which renew humanity,' Nandini gently reminded her. The years her father had spent teaching her the Mahayana sutras and scriptural teachings of Buddhism never failed her, as was the case with all her subjects of study.

'Yes, yes. I meant the same thing. Is that all that my detached-from-the-world brother has taught you? Spiritual inclinations are all very well, but being so wrapped up in his own world, he has failed to arrange a suitable marriage for you,' her aunt said, reaching out to embrace Nandini and drowning her in her ample bosom. 'I don't want you to despair. Your aunt is still alive; I will ensure you hook an eligible man before your eighteenth year commences.'

Nandini, meanwhile, was trying to come up for air.

Very used to her aunt's matchmaking propositions, she never took them seriously. She disentangled herself, careful not to crease her full lehenga, which still felt awkward, almost clumsy, compared to the flimsy, pleated Patiala pyjamas and fine cotton kurtas she was so used to wearing in Lahore.

'I am so proud of my handiwork, you look like a woman now,' her aunt said, admiring Nandini's muslin lehenga and chiffon blouse. 'You should have been taught to dress like a lady years ago, but we both know, after my darling sister-in-law passed away, my brother left no stone unturned in bringing you up like a boy.' She continued, mistaking the frown marring Nandini's face—on account of her lehenga getting stuck between her legs—as displeasure at her upbringing. 'You have nothing to worry about, my dear, I will make sure you are well versed with all that is required to be accepted in society; even arrange for you to be married here, to a suitable boy of course—someone with at least two havelis, a hundred bighas of green land, a few villages, and who is well placed in the maharaja's army. Truth be told, I started receiving proposals long before you got here, but the mothers are wary of your fiery, tomboyish nature. Nothing we cannot fix.' She beamed at her niece.

Nandini refused to comment; she had been through this conversation several times before, and had learnt to agree with her aunt instead of answering back. The sooner her so-called transformation was complete, the sooner she could return to her father in Lahore.

Shreyas Kanwar, or the Thakurani of Trilok, as she insisted on being called, had made it her occupation to mind everyone else's business.

Twenty years ago, she had caused a small scandal, accomplished by marrying a forty-eight-year-old trader from Trilok, one of Rajputana's wealthiest and most influential trading houses. Overnight, she traded her severe, unvarnished muslin lehengas for resplendent lengths of brocades embroidered with silver, and organzas so feathery, they felt like butter on skin; pearls that equalled the Maharani of Baroda's; and diamonds handpicked from the heart of Golconda. Having secured for herself a rich but, unfortunately, untitled husband, Shreyas had shifted her attention to the more pressing matter of contriving a fictitious title to match her new-found riches, and had reinvented herself as the thakurani. Over the years, she had mastered the fine art of spending her husband's money on acquiring the latest designs in silk and investing in silverware, when she wasn't hosting lavish dinner parties in an attempt to ascend Jaigarh's very steep social ladder.

Nandini turned around, busying herself in spreading out red chillies to dry in the central courtyard. She had left behind all that was familiar—weekend trips to Lahore to buy castaway books from the street vendors; verdant boulevards looping like circus clowns; the crumbling mansion in Multan; but most of all she missed her father—his calm voice and intellect as he diligently explained Emperor Akbar's position when his son Salim pronounced himself king and turned rebellious; the effect it had on the political situation in the country—even though Akbar managed to suppress the revolt, the father–son relationship had become highly strained—or while reciting one of the seven-hundred-odd verses in the ancient Sanskrit text of the Bhagavad Gita. This was another world of glitzy festivities, where women paraded around like peacocks dancing in the rain, desperately trying to entrap privileged, powerful partners; and of secrets and scandals, fuelled by inflaming gossip and malicious prattle—a world completely different from hers.

Her aunt had already taken the trouble to do so much for her, though. She would try and adapt. Turning briefly, Nandini smiled widely for her aunt's benefit and resumed the task at hand. Nandini had already been in Jaigarh for twenty days, but neither her aunt nor her cousin spoke of the genuine reason for her having to leave her beloved father and Lahore behind. They had buried it under layers of excuses, her aunt claiming that she and Devika longed for companionship in their 'colossal haveli'. Nandini knew they were doing their best to rescue her from her not-so-ideal situation.

Things hadn't fallen apart one fine day; they rarely did. After her mother had died giving birth to her, her father had never bothered himself with the running of the estate choosing, instead, to spend his days reading and raising his daughter in the village of Multan. He was magnanimous and generous with the bonded labourers, allowing them to share the profits, unlike his cavalier, condescending neighbours. Unfortunately, he had fallen into a severe financial crisis when an extended period of drought, coupled with a bad harvest, had exposed the family estate to peril. The crafty Mughal amir of their zila, Jung Bahadur, had seen this calamity as a favourable stroke of fortune. He arrived shortly, to advance his shelter and guardianship in exchange for Nandini's hand in marriage.

Nandini, however, found the amir, who was old enough to be her father, the most repulsively loathsome of all her admirers. He had already been married the four times permitted by Muslim law, but a few days before his ardent proposal, his oldest wife had mysteriously disappeared. Doubly alarmed, Nandini's father had dismissed the proposition, but this only seemed to make the amir chase her with renewed vigour.

Enraged, Nandini had declared to her father that she would rather marry the most impoverished pauper in Lahore than marry the pot-bellied, lecherous amir. Finally, things had reached a standstill last year, when half the town had gathered in Lahore, at the wedding of one of the amir's daughters to a powerful zamindar. When, on this occasion, the amir had renewed his proposal and asked for Nandini's hand in public, she had declined vehemently, yet again.

Not one to give up, the amir pursued her, and so a few months earlier, Nandini had challenged her paramour to a sword fight, and won. The bruised amir had gone back swearing revenge, and revenge he did get. He forged papers confiscating her father's estates and furthermore, stopped regular water supply to the remaining fields.

Meanwhile, news of the spitfire's beauty spread to most Rajput kingdoms. A lack of riches, coupled with a fiery disposition, did nothing to further her chances in the marriage market, much to the dismay of her father and aunt. So her aunt had invited Nandini to live with her after a lot of arm-twisting and emotional blackmail directed at her father; she had said she would get this niece of hers to behave like a respectable girl and secure her future. As a consequence, in a matter of days, the motherless girl had gone from horse riding with village boys to attending parties with noblewomen. The women seemed to be the larger beasts, thought Nandini wickedly.

Her thoughts were interrupted by her aunt's booming voice.

'Now girls, tonight is a big night. And I want you to look perfect,' Shreyas Kanwar said, tutoring her niece and daughter in the art of beautification. 'We don't want people to get the idea that we are not as wealthy as we give the impression of being. The idea is to look ethereal, like a fragile nymph crying out to be taken care of. Don't overdo it; we don't want you looking like some of these overdressed tarts, Devika.'

Devika giggled. She was threading pearls into her long black braid, and gave no attention to her mother's words, encasing her wrist with an uncut ruby bracelet. 'That should be difficult,' she said. 'The boy's mother adorns herself with enough precious baubles to give jewellers a run for their money. I saw her at my friend's house on Deepawali, and she was more lit up than all the diyas put together. We even placed bets on how long she would take to double over from the sheer weight of those ornaments.'

'Devika, a well-bred young lady would never speak like that, and I am beginning to be convinced you are not one. If you don't stop that incessant chatter at once, I will have to insist on another hour of hymn recital, every Tuesday of the coming moon cycle.'

Devika sat down, her face sulky.

'Tonight, I want both you girls to look as radiant as lotus buds and as innocent as doves begging to be captured,' the thakurani went on. She approached her daughter fondly; Devika, whom she had dressed in canary yellow and parrot green, all of this trimmed with pink, looked apprehensive. 'So remember to behave according to the golden rules. When I was your age, I had already acquired three havelis and an affluent husband, so tonight I want you to meet someone—no wait, let me finish—he is rich, eligible, and most of all, titled—a thakur. I cannot believe my daughter will finally be a thakurani,' she said, wiping away a melodramatic tear. 'Now, undeniably, there will be expectations, but when he sees you dressed in your colours...they are his children's favourites.' She saw the girls' faces. 'Oh, did I forget to mention he was previously married? Luckily, she died last month, leaving three children behind, but don't worry, there will be lots more; he is only forty—you will have your hands full.'

'I am too young to get married and even if I wasn't, I will never end up getting married if you make me wear that,' Devika protested, suspiciously eyeing the multicoloured mithai-like dress her mother had forced on her.

'Devika, how many times have I told you—we mothers know best. I am always right about these things; and look how it makes your dusky skin look brighter!'

'Why can't I just dress in plain old tissue?'

'Oh that look is so last century—dowdy and old-fashioned, like my mother-in-law. This is the latest fashion, you know; the Portuguese memsahibs wear the same fabrics. Now don't fuss; I know you are getting nervous and fidgety because you are dying to meet your thakur, ei?'

'Ma hukum...noooo...'

'Oh it's natural at this age to get all breathless and fluttery. Quiet, now. Go on both of you,' said the thakurani in a stern voice. 'It makes life so much easier when one doesn't open one's mouth.'

'Like puppets, you mean?' Nandini offered, cheekily.

The thakurani ignored the comment completely. 'Now, remember my golden words. You must act demurely—like a vision. Both of you, like the virgins you are. And remember, as a breed, men are very insecure, so no looking at anything male; not the eighty-year-old cook, not the parrot, not even the painting on the wall.'

Devika grimaced. Nandini nodded obediently, grimacing inwardly.

'Now listen carefully. In a nutshell, do your khamaginis till your back aches, do not look up or make direct eye contact even if it means falling into the tray of gulab jamuns, direct your gaze to the toes of his jootis, and in no case should you speak until you are spoken to.'

'In short, do not be yourself!' Nandini exclaimed.

'Good girl,' her aunt said, uncertainly.

She added, 'I think you may look him in the eye for the briefest of a second, but do not stare at him boldly like a street whore; quickly drop your eyes, and in no case should you scratch his eyes out with a sword as you did with Sukh Singh in Lahore—what a fine chap; pity the alliance didn't work out.' Both young ladies smothered their laughter.

'Oh, was he the one you challenged to a raan-eating competition or the one you scared off with tales of the haunted haveli in Sarika?' Devika held her sides in an attempt to contain her laughter.

'Enough, I think they are here now. Girls, remember everything I have told you.'

With that, the thakurani walked away towards the main door, eager to welcome her guests.

The festivities were in full swing. The haveli glowed with colour; only two young women seemed untouched by all of it.

'Oh dear, even the plague is preferable to this,' Nandini moaned.

'Nandini, look! There's your mother-in-law to be,' teased Devika.

'The plump one with peacock feathers stuck on her lehenga? She looks like a pudding.'

'Nandini, forget her face—just look at the size of those rubies and sapphires on her neck and arms! And her tissue pouch is stuffed with gold mohurs.'

'Khamagini, padhariye. I am so glad you could come,' said the thakurani to a guest in a shimmering red poshaak and a matching pouch and jootis. 'You look lovely. The colour suits you so well—makes you look not a day over forty—positively youthful.'

'What do you mean, not a day over forty? I am only thirty er...six.' The lady was not amused.

'Oh, sorry, I meant thirty—not a day over thirty,' the thakurani said placatingly.

'Just the other day, somebody mistook me for my husband's daughter,' trilled the guest, now appeased.

'By the way, has the Thakur of Sarika arrived yet?' asked her hostess.

'I haven't seen him, but he should be here soon,' the lady in red said, looking around the durbar hall. 'Where is the alcohol, Shreyas? I am dying for a drink.'

'Devika, go fetch us some drinks, please.' She smiled at the guest. 'My daughter always insists on serving my guests. She is perfect wife material.'

'Devika, darling, see that the drinks are served, and I don't want you sampling the alcohol. We can't afford to have you passing out near the cowshed like last time. And if you do decide to taste it, just take one tiny sip. I imagine the thakur will ask you to marry him tonight and I don't want you tipsy when he does,' she whispered to her daughter in a silvery voice, pinching her cheeks to add colour to them. 'There, now you look like a blushing bride to be.'

Devika recognized the opportunity and swiftly slipped away, rolling her eyes skywards, she had had exactly half a flute of some bitter fiery liquid that had been thrust into her hand by a matchmaking aunt to give her an air of sophistication around much older prospective grooms but she had found herself thoroughly intoxicated a few minutes after gulping the liquid and had passed out rather dramatically on her way to her set of suites. Her mother had never let her live the embarrassment down.

'Thakur of Sarika...'

The name drifted across the room, like a ring of smoke, reaching Devika who instantly turned round to identify the man behind the title. Her gaze stopped on an averagely tall man standing with his back towards her. He wasn't bald or fat or...ugly, she realized as he turned gradually towards her; he was quite handsome actually.

The man looked up and looked straight at her, a faint smile at the corner of his mouth. Oh my god, it was Manvendra...of course her mother hadn't mentioned his name. She knew Devika despised him. She would rather die a virgin—a prospect she wasn't keen on at all, she had to confess—than marry Manvendra. The cheek, to propose to someone as young and breathtakingly beautiful as her, or so she thought, when he obviously was a widower saddled with three children. So he wasn't a lecherous old man with half his teeth missing, maybe even pleasant on the eyes, but that didn't change anything—she had no intention of playing nursemaid to his children while he painted the kingdom red with his harem of whores...'escorts'.

Mustering up all her courage, she walked up to him and declared, 'Hukum, I know you're titled, rich, not so bad looking, and surprisingly well kept. Really, you need to tell my mother the secret of your youthful looks but...' she paused, 'I refuse to marry you. Nothing personal, it's just that I want to be swept away in love. I'm not greedy, though. I'm not bothered about him being a maharaja. A raja or a zamindar would do—but I refuse to play nanny to your brood of brats.'

Manvendra stared at Devika as if she were a madwoman on the loose.

'Youthful looks? What do you mean youthful looks? I am only twenty-nine. What brood are you talking about?' he asked incredulously.

'I know this is a terrible blow to your fragile ego, but I can't sacrifice my flower-like existence and crush my dreams to marry you. So I beg you to reject this proposal.'

'Marry you?' he laughed. 'Do you think I have lost my mind to send a proposal to marry you?'

Devika stilled in shock, then blinked. 'What? Don't you want to marry me?'

'Can a man fly? Can a cat talk? Can a woman ever talk sense? No, the answer is no—I have no intention of marrying you However, if you had something... shall we say less stifling in mind, I wouldn't actually mind your very indecent proposition. But marriage? Really, Devika, I thought you would be above throwing yourself at me, begging me to marry you. You must be desperate.'

'How dare you! You...you chauvinist pig! And your poor children! Refusing to acknowledge their presence to impress impressionable young women like me—how low have you sunk? And just because I have refused to marry you, that doesn't mean you lie through your teeth. My mother has told me a million times a proposal from the Thakur of Sarika...'

'Your mother? The less said about her...Did you say the Thakur of Sarika?' he said with a naughty twinkle in his eye. 'Shame on you, Devika, propositioning men. Though if you end up marrying the Thakur of Sarika I won't blame you,' he said, speaking very loudly now as if he were explaining something to a senile eighty-year-old woman.

'I am not the Thakur of Sarika,' he continued.

'But I heard his name—'

'My manservant wanted to be excused because the Thakur of Sarika has been proposing indecent things to him. Nothing to worry about though, rumour has it that he swings both ways,' Manvendra said, lowering his eyes to the hideous poshaak she was wearing. 'Nice outfit,' he winked.

Devika flushed a deep crimson. She was not sure

why Manvendra was affecting her at all. 'Excuse me, I have an urgent matter to attend to,' she said haughtily, mustering whatever leftover dignity she could before turning on her heel and walking out of the door.

'Devika, I have been looking everywhere for you, where do you keep vanishing? Now child—here is your lucky chance. The thakur is approaching us. Look down and act coy.'

Devika took one look at the bald, stubby, morbidly obese thakur. He could have been anywhere from fifty to sixty-five. She turned and announced to her mother, 'I have decided to become Buddhist, I will dedicate my life to serving others.' Grinning, she walked off to find her cousin, leaving a mortified mother behind.

Nandini had not fared any better. For the first time in her seventeen years of existence, she was being 'shown off'. She was squashed on the hanging brass swing, between the prospective groom's mother—whose girth required most of the seat—and her pregnant, restless daughter, who appeared to be in possession of a never-ending supply of opium. The groom's mother was all rolling eyeballs, flared nostrils and knitted brows; and very much in a one-sided conversation with the portly pandit who sat cross-legged, opposite them, and snored constantly, adding considerably to the varying degrees of shrill female chatter. The pregnant woman next to her talked unceasingly to anyone unfortunate or unwise enough to make eye contact with her—in this case, Nandini.

'Now, I am not one of those women who will praise themselves, but I must tell you what a catch my brother is. I receive a dozen proposals for Lakshya every day—someone offers us a palace; others promise us cartloads of rice all the way from Vijayanagaram, and a dozen camels. Oh the list is endless, but Lakshya took one look at you and insisted he must marry you.'

Nandini's mind was far away. She leaned back against the cool brass of the swing, praying the silver zardozi wouldn't cut into her skin. Yet for all the discomforts of the intricately embroidered ensemble that left her back red and her arms scratchy, she was not in the least inclined to leave the party. She had just left behind the lifelong familiarity of Lahore, her home, and family, and did not want to shame her father in front of her aunt and her relatives. Also, her aunt had been generous and kind, and she lived like a pampered guest rather than a poor relative. It was for these reasons that she behaved.

Also, her Dai ma had scared her with stories of spinsters living with cats on isolated farms, and had made it very clear that Nandini could expect only dreariness and drudgery ahead, if she didn't mend her ways. She would end up as one of those lonely, barely-there women, always dressed in black, working as an unpaid servant to a bunch of ungrateful relatives. Maybe she would just be left alone to read in her haveli, she thought. But what of passion, what of stolen kisses, the kind that Shivendra had planted on her lips? Looking around the room, it became clear to her that there was no one else she was attracted to, no one she could feel that passion with. She would have to be a mistress to a man like him; that was the only other option, it seemed. She smiled mirthlessly.

The determined pregnant woman next to Nandini interrupted her thoughts.

'Now don't be shy, go show Lakshya your face; he has been talking only about you ever since he spotted you at the wedding.'

Nandini got up, standing still for a moment to balance the weight of the gold ornaments piled on her, before walking to the other end of the room. There, Lakshya had seated himself on an ivory bench.

Before she had a chance to bend low and greet him, she felt his hand tug her wrist, his dark eyes glittered with mischief as he lounged back on the bench, hooking one lean leg over its elaborately carved arm, as if he already owned her and the haveli. From the corner of her eye she spied her perturbed aunt, frantically fanning herself in spite of the cool of the satin fans. He took a lazy sip of alcohol, emptying his goblet and studying her from top to bottom in one brazen look. 'Nandini, you get prettier every time I see you, like a lotus blooming especially for me; no, don't lower your eyes—they are as intoxicating as the alcohol that I sip.'

'I thank the zamindar for his compliments.' Nandini smiled sweetly and prepared to rise.

'Don't leave just yet, I haven't even starting complimenting your bounteous charms. Here's to our future, Nandini.' His gaze lowered to the level of her kurti, his very own salacious accolade to her charms. He was definitely drunk.

Nandini grit her teeth behind a gracious smile. 'May I offer you some more alcohol?'

'Of course. Alcohol served by someone as beautiful as you—I'd feel like I died and went to a celestial harem.' Nandini picked up the crystal canister, and closing her fingers, stiff with outrage, around its silver handle, tipped it over, draining the amber liquid on his head.

'Mad woman! Have you lost your mind?' He sprang to his feet, drenching the Persian rugs with a stream of alcohol.

'I beg your forgiveness, Thakur hukum. My nervousness makes me so clumsy.' She gave him a knowing look and turned around—only to find her aunt, frozen like one of the sculptures in the room.

Her aunt's horrified scowl warned her she had gone too far this time. 'You must forgive my niece, Thakur. She's been troubled by the loss of her mother and has never recovered completely.' Shreyas hastened to add, 'Nothing permanent or hereditary, of course,' before flapping around the room, waving a piece of silk at Lakshya's mother as a gesture of truce.

Lakshya shoved the offending goblet away, eyes angry. Nandini looked away. She had no regrets. Men who treated women like playthings weren't worth respecting.

'Maybe you should invite me after treating your unstable niece first. I must take your leave before I do something I will regret, khamagini,' Lakshya said, walking out of the room.

'Really, Nandini, must you be so clumsy? I don't know what to do with you,' said her aunt, looking at her niece sorrowfully. Nandini turned around and ran up the stairs to her room.

Later, when the evening was drawing to a close, the thakurani found her wayward niece. She sat on the divan opposite her, looking reprovingly at Nandini. She snapped open her paandaan and vigorously started preparing a paan for herself. She only ate paan when she was very annoyed.

'Nandini, what you did today was very shameful. How could you! Lakshya is so upset. Why do you keep behaving like this? What did you say to Zamindarni sahiba? Nandini, I am asking you if you told the zamindarni you were...shameful as it is to even say...barren?'

Nandini popped a gulab jamun in her mouth and shook her head. She had no viable explanation for her behaviour earlier that evening; something had clicked suddenly and try as she might, she couldn't play the part of devoted, sugarcane-sweet, prospective daughter-in-law. This was easier and anyway, she was just following her aunt's instructions. After all, as her aunt was so fond of repeating, a lady should never speak with her mouth occupied by anything other than her tongue.

'Such an honourable lady, she promised me this unfortunate...news will go with her to the grave, wouldn't believe me when I told her you had played a prank,' she paused for a sceptical snort. 'How on earth could you offend the mother of your most eligible suitor?' Her aunt glowered at her. 'And don't get me started about the Raghuvanshi family, they have six havelis, not simple houses, but large havelis, all marble inlaid with real gold filigree; even their servants eat in silver thalis, and what did you do? You faked a dreadful disease and spilt sticky sweetmeats on the plume in the zamindarni's favourite hat from London, that hat cost as much as three camels!'

Nandini swallowed the gulab jamun. 'She did look like a rather obnoxious bird of paradise in it, with that ridiculous purple-and-red hat matching her fuchsia poshaak.'

'You have no idea about style and fashion; hats are all the rage, from Agra to Amritsar. The next time the junior commanding officer goes back to England, I must ask his wife to get one each for both of you,' her aunt said thoughtfully. 'It's not your fault my dear, nobody can have any sophistication and refinement growing up in Multan.'

'But you grew up there,' blurted Nandini, speaking before thinking, as usual. Her aunt looked at her piercingly. When she had gathered enough composure to speak, her voice was dangerously calm. 'If it is the only thing I do, I will make sure you are married before the end of this full-moon cycle.'

Nandini heard a new forcefulness in her aunt's voice, and looked up, surprised.

Her aunt put both her hands up, as if beckoning the gods to drive sense into her niece's empty head. 'Girls your age are preparing to look for suitable matches for their daughters; everyone wants a fourteen-year-old wife. What are you waiting for? If you like someone, tell me, or tell your father, but don't give us sleepless nights by insulting prospective grooms like this. You test my patience, my dear. Just remember, your beauty is temporary, and once that goes, you will be left with nothing.' With that, she rose from the divan, gathering the skirts of her poshaak and sweeping across the stone floor. 'You have no idea what it is to have an unwedded girl in the house, I can't sleep, I can't eat, it's a curse!'

Nandini stood silently, staring at the painting of goddess Kali that adorned the wall. She was truly sorry for hurting her aunt's feelings like this, but she felt smothered and suffocated; every time she stepped out in the sun, there was someone to admonish her for not veiling her face; if she sat out in the sun eating mandarins on a sunny morning, someone would tell her to sit in the shade lest she blemish her flawless colouring; and, heaven forbid, if she ever laughed out loud, her aunt would lecture her and brand her unladylike.

Unaware of the conflict going on in Nandini's mind, Shreyas turned to her and announced, 'I promised your mother on her deathbed that you would marry, and marry you shall. Whom are you waiting for? There are no perfect men, no happily-ever-afters, so stop living in this world of dreams and embrace reality. I want you to marry the next man I choose for you, and I expect you to respect my wishes. Good night, my child.'

A fierce desperation rose in Nandini's heart. Was she to be sentenced to a loveless existence in a morbid haveli with a man she had no interest in? Were all of her unspoken dreams, of riding into the sunset with her soulmate, to rot to dust?

Sinking to her knees on the narrow latticed balcony, she skimmed the endless dunes of silver below her, piled like waves in an ocean, and the craggy dark peaks of the arid Aravali hills.

The scent of sweet jasmine engulfed her senses as tears trickled down her cheeks.

'What am I waiting for?' she repeated.

Devika walked in and seated herself by Nandini's side. Both sisters looked out at the full moon, which was painting the landscape silver.

'I've decided to become an old maid,' Nandini said to her cousin between sniffs.

'You can't do that.' Devika laughed.

'Why not?'

'Because if you do, you'll be penniless. You won't be able to have khoya pedas or lal maas, you'll have to live on puffed rice and chickpeas.'

'Chickpeas? Oh, I hate chickpeas. In that case, it is settled—I would rather marry a halwai than marry that lecherous Lakshya or become a nanny to someone's kids.' Nandini sniffed.

All of a sudden, an image of Shivendra as she had seen him last, looking at her before she turned around and ran, came into her head.

'Why does Shivendra fluster me so?' she wailed out loud, much to her sister's confusion. 'I care neither for his rank nor his wealth. He is everything I have dreamt of, bewitchingly handsome, powerful.' Nandini went on, not giving Devika a chance to speak.

'Yes, I know that he is also a womanizer, an arrogant playboy. And yes, what he offered was an indecent proposal. But Devika, he is so...oh, this is terrible, I think I am falling in love with him! What have I got myself into?' she said, sobbing into her silk handkerchief.

'Yes, his offer was indecent. And he was also rude and arrogant,' Devika reminded her cousin. Her mother had had a long talk with her and implored her to advise her cousin wisely. 'And there'll be other men. Your lineage is impeccable, and sonnets praising your beauty have already reached faraway lands, if rumour is to be believed—lands you have yet to explore. You will forget and move on, especially with children to look after.'

Nandini grew silent again. She sat alone for a while, out on the balcony. By the time she went to bed, she was exhausted by the events of the day. Dismissing her dai, she undressed herself. Slipping out of the fineries that her aunt had decked her out in earlier that evening, she washed her face with a paste of sandalwood and ice-cold rose water, quelling some of the puffiness her face had suffered by virtue of her crying fit.

Finally, she sat alone in her room. The peacock suite, named appropriately after the peacocks that danced during the monsoons in all their glory, on the sandstone chattris lining the edges of the terrace. Free.

Sometime soon, she thought, just before she drifted off to sleep, she was going to have to start looking seriously at marrying some dull zamindar. It was either that, or becoming mistress to the yuvraj.

CHAPTER FOUR

'She rejected me,' Shivendra repeated, as if willing himself to believe those words. The words left a sourness in his mouth that he just couldn't rinse off. Shivendra, proud Yuvraj of Jaigarh, took another large gulp of the amber-coloured alcohol that had been gifted to him by a chieftain in Persia, after he had vanquished his fiefdom. He had been laden with presents of precious stones and riches, alcohol, gold, wanton and willing women—women who had danced around a bonfire in diaphanous robes, eager to please his every whim and fancy, unlike Nandini.

Nandini was a mere commoner, at the end of the day, and she had dared to turn him down. He fumed. She had the audacity to condemn his offer, spurn his advances; why, everything! His illustrious label, his colossal fortune, his coffers full of gold, and the privileges granted to her for being the chosen one. The chance to be the royal mistress was not to be taken lightly. And he wasn't an unattractive prospect; if a series of wide-eyed, besotted women were to be believed, his skills behind closed doors were perhaps the best aspect of this position. He lacked nothing and yet, she had rejected him. The three words he had uttered out loud, finally, were like hot coals on his tongue, burning fiercely. Even an entire bottle of alcohol could not dispel his fury.

'Dinner has been reheated and served, Hukum. How long do you wish for the coals to heat the meal, Hukum?' the servant boy asked timidly.

'I am not hungry,' Shivendra said, his face rigid. 'And I don't want any of you to disturb me.' He poured more alcohol into a gold-rimmed crystal goblet and gulped it down. He wanted to drink enough to forget all about Nandini, but her doe-like brown eyes kept dancing in front of him. He had eaten nothing since midday, but he could not stomach a morsel of the royal feast that awaited him.

'You must eat something, Hukum. I fear you will fall ill, you hardly touched lunch as it is,' attempted the boy again, at the risk of having an elephant tooth or a turquoise frame thrown at him. The boy was used to Shivendra's moods; he had been especially trained by the maharani, Shivendra's mother, to oversee his meals and comfort. Unfortunately for him, now was not the time to exhibit any sort of compassion for the yuvraj.

'Remove yourself from my sight,' Shivendra said through gritted teeth. The boy shrank back, with folded hands.

Shivendra glowered at the empty canister of scotch in his hand and walked to the ebony bar, uncorking another bottle of the intoxicating liquor. For a second his eye caught his reflection, standing amidst the opulence of the hall. The cultivated elegance of his surroundings confronted him. Yet there was a stark austerity about the palace, a void so dismal that it craved human warmth. He looked around and decided he would finally arrange for Ayesha Begum to shift to the palace zenana, a move he had long been resisting. There was nothing a woman's touch couldn't rectify.

Just then, a servant boy walked in to announce the arrival of a visitor. Shivendra scowled further when he heard Manvendra's familiar voice echoing through the royal corridors. For a minute, he had thought it was Nandini, sending word that she had changed her mind—not that he would pardon her insolence.

He thought of her cascading, silky hair, tresses that looked like midnight in the sun...No.

...and the sun-kissed, flawless skin that appeared to have been lit from within...

Not even if she begged and pleaded.

He had his pride, he was the Yuvraj of Jaigarh after all.

...and the swell of her breasts that begged to be released from the fine muslin constraining them...

He would decline to receive her, refusing even an audience with her.

A minute later, Manvendra came striding into the room through the arched hallway, instantly taken aback to find Shivendra staring into a half-empty glass of scotch. He sat down silently. He knew better than to anger Shivendra further in his present mood.

Shivendra glanced at his old friend then gestured for him to help himself from the bar. Striding across the room, Manvendra unstoppered a crystal decanter, pouring its contents into a tumbler which he gulped down in one go, and reached for the decanter again.

'It appears to me that you have had reason to be celebrating all night long,' Shivendra observed, his glance running the length of the velvet sherwani and opal buttons Manvendra had on.

'None that I can think of, unless you call being matchmade for by over-enthusiastic chuckling mothers a reason to celebrate. I spent the evening at Devika's house. Her mother makes our mothers seem like angels. She had Nandini sandwiched between Lakshya Singh and his equally obnoxious sister, while Devika was being paraded in front of the ancient Thakur of Sarika.'

Shivendra's fingers tightened around the neck of the canister involuntarily. 'Lakshya Singh? That worthless alcoholic? Why, he isn't even worthy enough to glance at her feet.'

'You can't blame her aunt; with not a single penny to her niece's name, she is desperate to wed her off to the first man that comes along,' Manvendra said, noting his friend's pursed lips. 'My mother mentioned that Lakshya insists he shall marry Nandini with or without a dowry—he proposed to her within a few minutes of laying his eyes on her.'

Shivendra paused and looked back at him, his eyebrows raised. 'But surely the fact that he is a pathetic drunkard will make Nandini reconsider? And don't even get me started about that sister of his, always smiling at me like a nun with a concussion.'

'Oh, she was there, plastered up like a buffalo caked with mud,' Manvendra said. 'Nandini's beauty does make her very...desirable to many; some would say she is the richest prize on the marriage market. I understand that her aunt expects to make an announcement any day.'

'Was a decision reached?' asked Shivendra, his voice giving no indication of the split-second turmoil that swept through him.

'None that I can see happening, Nandini poured a canister of alcohol over Lakshya's head. After that, I think there might be some fireworks in that house. Her aunt isn't going to mar an alliance with someone as rich as Lakshya even if he is the biggest drunkard in Jaigarh.'

Shivendra smiled, amused despite himself. He could just imagine the chaos that had ensued from Nandini's impulsive actions. Yet another transgression from Lahore's beautiful firebrand. But it looked like she would be tamed by Jaigarh society before he could get near her.

Manvendra took on the unspoken subject that lay between them. 'Judging by the expression on your face, you haven't had a very pleasant evening either. Is it the maharaja ordering you to marry well and beget an heir, or is it Nandini's charms that have your nerves as tightly wound as a whirring loom?'

'My mood has nothing whatever to do with the maharaja or Nandini,' snapped Shivendra. 'When I do marry, it will be because I want to, and not because I have to please the maharaja. As for Nandini, she is like a perfect pearl, one that I look forward to tarnishing. She entertains me, that chit of a girl—she is fiercer than the holy fire one moment and as cool as an ice princess the next. At least I won't suffer from boredom.'

'Well, if you don't marry and beget an heir in the near future, the maharaja will have every woman in Rajputana, single, widow, or spinster, under the age of thirty, lined up for you to choose from,' his friend said, laughing.

'Perish the thought. But if you must know, I intend to marry entirely to suit myself. I'm thirty and have no intentions of binding myself to the headache that is marriage just as yet.' That fate would never be his, Shivendra vowed. 'Marry I must, but I shall delay it for as long as possible, and then settle for an arranged alliance with a well-bred, dull woman who will bear my heirs, ask no questions and expect no answers. Someone who would be content to live in the zenana and be visited once or twice a year; someone who would produce a son to take over my kingdom; someone who would quickly fade into the background of my life. Not someone as beautiful as Nandini, beautiful women like her are invariably vain and fiery.'

'I can't say I am jealous; your ideal woman sounds awfully like my forty-year-old spinster aunt, an option that I am not keen to explore.' Manvendra walked towards the crystal lamp, then stopped short to stare at his reflection in the carved ivory mirror. 'That reminds me, we are getting older, let's go pay a visit to Ayesha Begum's kotha. There is a new girl there—Zahreen—whom I have taken a fancy to. I had better go and enjoy myself while I still can.'

He turned around to face his friend. 'You have a lot of explaining to do—you have been neglecting Ayesha Begum for far too long. Keep ignoring her summons and it won't be long before she latches on to some other nizam. There aren't many who can afford her, and of those, there are few that she would cast a second look at.'

'Two pieces of silver? This is daylight robbery. I am not going to pay more than one.' Devika picked up a turquoise and amethyst necklace and opened her silk pouch to pull out the payment. The cousins were shopping for jewellery in Jaigarh's busy marketplace.

'Nandini, do you like this?' Devika asked, holding the bauble to her neck. 'Nandiniii! Stop fiddling with your odhna and tell me if you like this?'

'Oho, this odhna! I can barely see beyond my next step. What colour is the necklace? My odhna is layering everything with green and yes, that includes your face.'

'You don't have to follow Ma hukum's instructions to the "t", just pretend that you do. Get rid of that veil. Perfect—isn't that so much more manageable?' Devika hiked up Nandini's veil and tucked it below the fold resting on her head. 'Just be careful it doesn't trail behind, or someone might step on it.'

'Look at this kamarbandh. It'll really accentuate your waist. Nandini, where is your attention? These merchants have come all the way from Hyderabad, look at these gems—pearls that are plump and shiny like just-kissed lips; sapphires that are darker than the midnight sky; and rubies richer than the sunset.'

'Forgive me. Jewels don't seem to be holding my attention today, but don't let me keep you from choosing what you want.'

'Nandini, is it Shivendra? Are you still thinking about him?'

'Of course not, I have barely met him. Eccentricities like love have no place in my life. It's just this silly veil. I think veils were invented by cheating husbands to prevent their wives from discovering their philandering ways.'

'Or by ageing mothers-in-law so they are not reminded of their young daughters-in-law's beauty!' Devika added, impishly.

Nandini laughed in spite of herself. She didn't want to lie to Devika. Her dear cousin was going out of her way to make sure she was comfortable, but she couldn't tell her the spell hadn't quite been broken yet. But it would soon go away. This was a frivolous infatuation, a complete waste of time and emotions. She was just another woman to have fallen for the yuvraj's charms. And even though she was attracted to him by an overwhelming magnetic force, she would rather die before he knew that. He was a yuvraj and she was a common girl. And she knew the social order did not permit alliances between a prince and a commoner.

Suddenly, she was aware of a great clamour from behind her; horses snorting and whinnying, men shouting. Then, in a flash of a second, something hard and solid bumped into her from behind, knocking her off balance. She landed unceremoniously on her bottom, her lehenga spread out around her. For a second, Nandini did not know what had hit her—was this the earthquake her father had warned her about? Everyone else looked normal, except for the fact that they were staring at her.

She looked up and she could see two horsemen directly ahead of her. One of them had dismounted his horse and was walking towards her. It was then that she realized she had been knocked over by a horse. If this was not enough, she was still sitting in the middle of the road, without a veil to protect herself from the crowd of common men ogling at her. Devika hurried towards her, helping her to her feet, and in the interim Nandini caught the merest glimpse of the man, cloaked in a velvet cape embroidered with silver.

It was the face that had haunted Nandini's memories. Here, before her, was the cause of her ignominious fall; the man who had caused her many sleepless nights, towards whom she now nursed a considerable hostility.

She seethed. Of all the incautious, irresponsibly hazardous things to do. Just because these men were royalty, did they think they could trample pedestrians? How heedless of them to endanger someone's life in their recklessness. Before she could collect herself sufficiently and rearrange her poshaak, a tanned arm clad in the softest muslin—she was surprised by its feel against her arm—reached out to steady her. She looked up to meet the yuvraj's face. Dark, deep, frowning eyes met her gaze.

Nandini ignored his hand and steadied herself, with all the dignity she could summon.

'This road might be your property, Yuvraj, but people's lives are not,' she said, above the din of the marketplace, her voice rising above the chatter of the people who had gathered around. 'The next time you decide to trample some unsuspecting commoner, please remember, justice in this kingdom is equal for all. A rule that your father, the maharaja, is famous for putting into practice.'

Shivendra had forgotten how beautiful she was. Even in this state of disarray, she looked like a goddess. The afternoon sun caught the sheen of her raven hair, turning it into a waterfall of glittering black diamonds, spilling liquidly over her shoulders. Her golden skin glinted with moisture, the silk of the peach lehenga that encased her lush womanly curves clung to her like a lover's arms. With a quick dart of her tongue over her lips, she opened her mouth. He found himself wondering how those lips would taste.

'I apologize, I was riding far too fast. A child came out running in front of me, and I had to swerve to avoid him. The horse got slightly unsettled and ran towards you. Looks like even my horse seems to have good taste.' Shivendra smiled at her, instantly transforming his rugged features from brooding to pleasant.

Thrown by his explanation and not a little

embarrassed, Nandini took him in: his strong muscular shoulders, broad chest, the manly frame encased in a cream muslin angrakha; all of him radiating raw power and sensuality.

'Blaming your horse for your less-than-perfect riding skills, Yuvraj? How the mighty have fallen,' she retorted, striving to keep her composure, her bottom still stinging from the fall.

'My riding skills are the best in the kingdom, a feat I am well prepared to prove...'

'Don't bother, Yuvraj,' Nandini cut in. 'I wouldn't dream of embarrassing the heir of Jaigarh. Why, it is improbable you could beat me at riding but we will let that go.'

'You go too far, curtail that viper-like tongue of yours Nandini, and never forget that you are addressing the yuvraj,' Manvendra interrupted.

'Who are you to tell me what I can say? I can only be asked to curtail my tongue, but the less said about the both of you, the better. Womanizing drunkards have no right to tell me what to do or not to do. I'm not some simpering, submissive woman from your kingdom who will bear every eccentricity coming from you, and don't forget that. Ever.'

'Nandini, stop overreacting. You are making too much fuss over this; let's leave. We have already created a scandal in the marketplace,' Devika whispered to Nandini. She was fighting her own sense of unease, not having expected to see Manvendra again so soon after her embarrassing misunderstanding. The man probably thought she was chasing him.

'I am not creating a fuss. And there is no way I am going to walk away from here without an apology from both of these arrogant aristocrats,' Nandini declared, not to be swayed.

Shivendra looked back at her disdainfully, with one eyebrow cocked. 'I have apologized once and that is the only apology you are getting, though you don't deserve even that.' He turned around and walked off towards his horse. Nandini pulled her veil down and stormed off in the opposite direction.

Vowing to forget all about the impudent Nandini, Shivendra rode off towards his mistress's house. By the time Shivendra arrived at the house he had bought for Ayesha Begum, it was already half past nine. Ayesha, who was overjoyed to see her most generous benefactor, immediately busied herself in serving the yuvraj fresh paan. She applied herself to the prince, keeping him busy until the first rays of sunlight swept into the room, but even her best efforts fell short. The yuvraj was distant and reserved, his mind was far away from the pleasure that her mouth was lavishing on him.

The next morning, after a hot bath, Ayesha paused and stared at her large almond-shaped eyes in a silver-framed full-length mirror that adorned the wall. She knew she was courted by half the men in Jaigarh, the other half of whom she had already bestowed her favour upon but she still needed to reassure herself that she was beautiful. What she saw in the mirror pleased her, her ivory skin was blemish free and luminous, maintained by a two-hour massage of pure saffron oil. She dropped her silk cover and gathering her hip-length mocha-coloured hair to one side, ran a critical eye down the length of her voluptuous body. Her waist was not as slim as it had been, no doubt the result of fattening food coupled with a lavish lifestyle, but her rounded breasts and bottom was where she had packed on the majority of weight. The men weren't complaining. She pinched the beige puffy nipples on her slightly sagging breasts and felt a tremor of pleasure pass through her body. She would just have to try harder, she thought, and prepared herself to face the yuvraj again.

Shivendra had retired to the mardana to look over some accounts and paperwork, but Ayesha was going to have none of it. She seductively placed herself on his lap, one delicate and determined hand slipping into his angrakha, the other loosening the ties of her own ensemble. It was only when a messenger interrupted them with a discreet cough that Shivendra looked up from his 'urgent' business concerns.

'I will be back shortly, go back to your chambers,' Shivendra said, trying desperately to get his mistress to cover herself. But Ayesha had been neglected too long and she refused to compromise.

Shivendra smiled easily. 'Darling, much as I would love to spend every waking moment in your arms, I do have other responsibilities.'

Ayesha pouted and sulked, still not ready to move. 'Why don't you get yourself a new necklace or that gold maang tikka you were talking about?' Ayesha's face lit up in excitement and she strutted off after hearing the magic words.

Breathing a sigh of relief, Shivendra turned to the messenger who was still standing by the door indifferently. 'What is it? I had left specific instructions not to bother me while I am here.' The messenger bowed low. 'Yuvraj, the maharaja has summoned you to the palace,' he said crisply. 'He wants you to be present at the durbar hall after lunch today.'

Shivendra paced the length of his study. If this was any of that business about getting married and begetting heirs he would have to set the record straight and make it very clear that there would be no bawling babies in the near future. The trouble with being a yuvraj was the kind of responsibilities that came with the title, responsibilities that he was born into. But he was determined to reap the benefits too; he would have Nandini yet. Truth be told, his plans had gone completely awry; his body still ached for Nandini. He could not put her out of his mind, try as he might.

CHAPTER FIVE

'SCANDALOUS!' CHANDRAVEER SINGH, THE minister sitting to the left of the maharaja, said one more time. 'I hear the yuvraj and his friends gamble and drink all night long, these are definitely not traits I want to see in the future maharaja.' He held up his hands as if asking the gods to intervene. 'And his "liaisons" with that—that courtesan—the less said about that, the better! How irresponsible of him to come so late. But what can one expect of Yuvraj Shivendra?'

'Khamagini, Maharaja.' Shivendra, who had just walked into the durbar hall of the palace, bowed low to the maharaja first, and then to the disgruntled minister. 'I apologize for arriving late; I was at the summer palace when I received the message and came as soon as I could. As for you, Chandraveer Singh, I believe I am doing you a mighty service, Hukum. At least I provide you with something to talk about. Perhaps it distracts you from the question of how you intend to keep the existence of your mistress a secret from your wife?'

Manvendra chuckled as the minister's face took on the colour of an overripe tomato. 'I believe the yuvraj has earned his place; he single-handedly threw the amir's enemy back to Ajmer six moons ago.'

'Six moons ago? Surely you can do better than that. In times of peace, it is impossible to tell who is deserving,' the minister said, not to be quelled for long. 'Maybe we should have some sort of parameter, not that I expect the yuvraj to prove himself.'

'Enough, Chandraveer Singh, I can smell the beginning of treason,' the maharaja interrupted him with a swish of his left hand. 'If you believe my son is not deserving, the yuvraj will prove himself to be worthy of the crown. Do you accept the challenge, Yuvraj?'

Shivendra raised his eyebrows. 'Maybe that's what I will do. Let's have a duel, a sword-fighting duel. I declare that the winner will be rewarded a thousand gold mohurs from my personal treasury, and the right to sacrifice the goat at the Ashtami puja, on the eighth day of Navratri.' And with that, he strode off in the direction of the main entrance with his soldiers in tow.

'Are you sure?' Manvendra asked, walking with him. 'What is the need to prove yourself to a mere minister?'

'Ah,' the yuvraj said carelessly, fastening his sword to the bronze belt on his waist. 'But I have to prove myself; it's his right to demand proof of my worthiness.' He frowned suddenly. 'I cannot afford to have any rebellions, however small and insignificant. The match will stop wagging tongues.'

'I shall order for notices proclaiming the challenge to be put up in the city square.'

'Yes, do that.' Shivendra lowered his voice as he mounted his horse. 'I may even find some able men from the villages to join my army. It is a period of peace, but you never know when the Mughals decide to attack.'

'What does the letter say, is all well at home, Nandini?' Devika asked, peering over her cousin's shoulder. Nandini was reading her father's letter for the umpteenth time. 'Does it say how much it will take to restore the estate?'

Nandini chewed her lower lip, lost in thought. 'I have no idea, Devika. Baba hukum hasn't mentioned it, but it is so like him not to share his problems with me.' She jumped off the brass swing and walked towards the marble fountain in the balcony, which, through a finely latticed curtain of stone, overlooked the Aravali range. 'It could take anywhere from six hundred to seven hundred gold mohurs to restore the estate, and another four hundred to six hundred to fertilize the farms so that the land starts paying for the estate's maintenance'.

'So...that is about thirteen hundred mohurs,' Devika said, doing the math.

Nandini's heart plummeted to her feet. To actually hear how much was owed was disheartening. She was the solution to the problem. She should be agreeing to marry someone suitably wealthy. But there had to be another way. She knew her aunt had offered to help, and that her self-respecting father had politely, yet firmly, refused to accept charity.

'I could sell off my mother's prized diamonds and my other pieces of jewellery, they could cover this,' Nandini said aloud, only realizing her folly when Devika protested, outraged.

'Nandini, that is your streedhan, your inheritance; and most importantly, your mother's memories are attached to each and every one of those pieces. I know those diamonds are worth a king's ransom, but they're all you have.'

'Baba flew into a rage the only time I suggested it. He promised my mother on her deathbed that I would wear them at my wedding, and I don't wish to be disrespectful to my mother's spirit, but Devika, I hardly knew her. My father needs help right now and it is just so...frustrating to be unable to help him.'

'I know, but when word gets out that you are trying to sell your mother's prized jewellery, people aren't going to stand by without defaming your father's reputation even further. How do you think he will react when people point fingers at him for making his daughter sell the family heirlooms? That would kill him, he is so proud.'

Devika stroked her cousin's hair and tried to console her. Rajputs placed pride before wealth or status. A woman was supposed to manage her household and bring up the children, not worry her pretty head about finances and land—the latter had always been a male domain.

Nandini bit her tongue to prevent herself from saying she did not care about her wedding or about wagging tongues. After the kindness she had been shown by her aunt and uncle over the past few months, it would be churlish to say how she longed to go back to Multan, to her beloved father. Her aunt was a kind woman, stripped of her brocades and kundan jewellery; she had to find a way out without letting her down.

'I'm sorry it's come to this, Nandini, but we will find a way out. Now cheer up. Listen—drumbeats!' Drums were used to convey special messages by the royal family to the people of Jaigarh. The men assembled at the square for the message ceremony, while the women listened to the proclamation from behind the purdah.

'You mean it's time for a royal sermon?' Nandini asked.

'Sermon? No, no, some time back, Yuvraj Shivendra had announced that he was exempting the farmers from the seasonal tax, since it hadn't been a good season for the crops. There was much rejoicing for the next three days. And then, at one time, a royal messenger was sent out at three in the morning to warn us about the Mughal invasion. It simply means a royal messenger will beat the drum and announce something of utmost importance in every section of Jaigarh.' Devika ran towards the open terrace excitedly, her crimson odhna fluttering in the wind.

'Nandini, come here, or you will miss the royal parade. Look, it must be something very important—there are six messengers instead of four.' Devika pointed towards the six messengers, dressed regally in royal blue angrakhas, their well-oiled moustaches proudly on display as they read out the royal message.

'Yuvraj Shivendra has challenged the residents of Jaigarh to prove their capabilities in a sword-fighting duel to be held in a fortnight. This contest is open to everyone, irrespective of caste or creed, and everyone who wishes to participate will be given a sword. The winner will receive a thousand gold mohurs from the yuvraj's personal treasury, and the right to sacrifice the goat on the eighth day of Navratri.'

'One thousand mohurs?' Nandini repeated in awe.

'Don't even think about it, this is not some game for us girls. You can't be serious, sword-fighting is dangerous. People get injured, even die sometimes. Forget you heard that message.' Devika took her cousin by the wrist and led her away.

What Devika didn't know was that Nandini was an expert swordswoman. She hadn't beaten the evil amir in their duel by chance; she had spent her childhood dressed in her father's oversized kurtas, chasing the village boys with her grandfather's rusty old sword. Finally her father had given in and taught her the basics of wielding a sword, a skill that she had honed by practising on childhood friends who had now been recruited into the amir's army. They still spoke of her reverently; she had them flat on the ground in less than three minutes.

Indeed, watching her fight with such gusto, Mohammad Anwar Ali, the acclaimed swordsman, had taught her some tricks. It was an honour to be trained by him. A legend in his time, he taught her to study the opponent's moves; every man had some flaw and if she paid attention to detail, she could pinpoint exactly when he would turn or which hand he used more. Nandini had never forgotten that piece of advice and had gone on to win every duel that she participated in. Since most competitions were closed to women, she would dress like a man, masking her lower face with the tail of the turban, which would hide her waist-length hair.

'Don't be silly, Devika, I wouldn't dream of doing something so foolish. Now let's go eat something, I'm famished.'

Devika frowned. She knew something was brewing in her cousin's mind. But later, while eating dinner, Nandini looked surprisingly calm and collected, and by the time the cousins went to sleep, Devika had forgotten all about the incident.

The next morning, Nandini bathed at dawn and coyly seated herself next to her bua in the puja room, which she spent the next hour cleaning and decorating with freshly plucked lotus pods. 'Nandini, my child, you are up early. Are you feeling unwell?' Shreyas Kanwar asked in concern.

'Unwell? Of course not, I thought it would be nice to wake up with the rising sun, like you always ask us to.' Nandini smiled at her aunt as she prepared the lamps to be placed around the tulsi plant in the core of the courtyard. 'Bua hukum, I have spent the last few nights thinking about what you said and I must ask you to forgive my immaturity. I think I need to devote myself to God in order to find a suitable husband. I have decided to go to the temple every day and do sewa for an hour till I am blessed with a husband, if I have your blessings that is.'

Shreyas Kanwar blinked disbelievingly at the niece who, just last month, had refused to accompany her to the temple or fast for Shiva's blessing. She looked at her niece suspiciously. She hadn't grown this old without realizing that a dog's tail could never be straightened. But here was her dear, wayward niece, transformed, beaming at her. Everybody deserved a second chance and maybe, just maybe, her talk had finally drilled some sense into the girl. A woman's touch could do wonders, and the Thakurani of Trilok wasn't just any woman.

'That sounds wonderful, my dear! And what an auspicious day to begin, its Lord Shiva's day—he is the lord of husbands, after all. If you pray to him, he will bless you with a husband as handsome as himself. Now run along and don't forget to carry a thali and some coconut...'

Nandini didn't wait for her aunt to finish. Gripping the sword that she had tucked into the recesses of her luggage in Multan, and clumsily tucking a thali and a coconut under her left arm, she headed across the town marketplace, towards the city auditorium. To her surprise, there was a long line of men clustered around the open field, cheering the contestants on.

Mentally asking the Lord to forgive her for this deception, she expertly wrapped the turban around her face and stood in the queue to wait her turn. The match had several elimination rounds, and during the first, she had to fight with a soldier from the army. After this, she would fight with the other opponents till she defeated them all. On the final day, she would have to compete with the best swordsmen in the competition—including the yuvraj.

The six-foot-three-inch-tall soldier eyed her slight frame with compassion. 'Are you sure you want to do this? You look undernourished and weak to me, go back home and eat a few roast lamb steaks and some bowls of ghee before you come back.' His answer was a swish of the sword that almost had him. Five minutes later he was lying on his stomach, the sand gritting into his teeth while the other swordsmen just stood and stared. For the rest of the practice, most men avoided Nandini, while the remaining few peered at her masked face with curious anticipation.

By the end of the session, she had been selected to compete on the final day, amidst much cheering by several onlookers. They had grown curious about the newcomer's identity.

Satisfied with the results of the match, Nandini hurriedly exchanged the turban for her odhna before exiting the auditorium from the back gate. She calculated the time; she still had ten minutes to get to the temple, ask God for his blessings and his forgiveness, and reach home before Devika got suspicious. That day, people were amused to watch a young veiled girl running the streets of Jaigarh as if an army of rats was chasing her. Fifteen minutes later, Nandini was sitting between her aunt and her cousin, glowing in a freshly washed turquoise lehenga, chomping on pieces of coconut from her puja.

'What made you change your mind, Nandini?' Devika eyed her cousin's breakfast plate jealously, between bites of her own fresh fruit and sweetened yogurt. Nandini was on her second helping; all that exercise had made her very hungry and she helped herself to yet another ghee-laden paratha and mawa barfi.

Nandini looked up. 'Oh...nothing, I just thought—can I have some more thickened milk?—just thought that maybe God will show me the right...mmm, this cottage cheese paratha is delicious. As I was saying, God will show me the right direction.'

'Just like that? I mean, out of the blue, you wake up one day and spend two hours at the temple singing hymns...you of all people?' Devika wasn't ready to give up yet. There was something not right about this situation.

'Devika,' her mother rebuked her, 'just because you are too lazy to pray and fast, don't spoil your sister. Instead of learning to be as devout as her, you are accusing her of being an agnostic like you. God knows one is bad enough!'

'Ma hukum, I just...'

'Enough, if you can't go to the temple, you will sit at home and recite the Bhagavad Gita for one hour every day. Look at Nandini, she is positively glowing, her soul is being blessed. With a pinch of help from me of course.'

'Ma hukum, that is not radiance oozing out of her

pores, it is ghee. Look, she's on her third paratha; she never eats so much. I am sure there is something fishy going on.'

'Devika, stop putting an evil eye on your cousin. She walked to the temple and back, she needs nourishment. And where is the bowl of ghee I had asked you to drink? How many times have I told you ghee will strengthen you and help you have lots of sons later in life?'

Shreyas picked up a bowl of freshly pressed ghee and added some gond to it. But when she turned around to force it down her unwilling daughter's throat, Devika had long disappeared from the scene of action. 'That girl! Here, Nandini, help yourself to more jalebis.'

Two weeks later, Nandini nervously approached one of the guards standing at the entrance of the palace. Too nervous to admire the grandeur of the palace, she rechecked her turban, securing it tightly around her face. The guard allowed her inside, where another guard escorted her through pristine lawns and into the yuvraj's private hall, now teeming with fifty-odd opponents who sparred as a growing audience looked on. Nandini took a deep breath and looked around her.

The durbar hall was palatial in dimension, grander than any palace that she had seen in Lahore; several times larger than her father had described. Its magnificent dome was painted ornately, in wine red and gold. Several plush divans, decorated with jewelled velvet, and elaborately carved wooden chairs were scattered around the room; silk carpets that had been delicately hand woven were thrown across the ochre sandstone floors; tasselled tapestries woven in pure gold were draped against the walls. The room held an array of pashmina throws, precious stone sculptures, and souvenirs from faraway exotic lands.

Yuvraj Shivendra was seated at the other end of the room. His damp angrakha clung to his finely sculpted torso. It was obvious he had been fighting opponents before this but he had a look of faint boredom on his face. A look that was both silent and arrogant.

Nandini glanced around the room till her sight settled on a tissue pouch, fat with gold mohurs. She stared at it with a hint of defiance in her dark eyes. It would be hers. This was her only chance to help her father; her life depended on that pouch.

The daydream was shattered by the blades of swords which clanged vehemently against each other; the room resonated with the echo of metal on metal. At one end, a man with a glass eye charged forward towards his opponent, his sword viciously wounding his opponent's torso while Manvendra fought off two aspirants with practised ease, at the other end. One of his challengers counter-attacked from the back, but he was quick to retreat a step and lunge back at the half-blind man.

Nandini ignored them. All her attention was focused on her opponent, a dark man with a wiry beard and stained teeth. She thanked God her identity was concealed by the tail of the turban that she had secured around half her face. A lot of soldiers chose to fight that way in the desert, to protect themselves from the blazing sun, and nobody paid her any attention. She tightened her hand on the hilt of her sword and pounced towards him, driving the full force of her sword into his and striking the sword out of his hand, in a matter of a few seconds. She moved on to the next contestant, and soon found herself settling into a steady rhythm as she went from one opponent to the other.

Attack, counter-attack, pounce, manoeuvre, evade. After defeating the next six adversaries, Nandini found herself facing none other than the yuvraj, who had been watching this vigorous new swordsman with interest. She had been meant to fight Manvendra before fighting with the yuvraj but Shivendra, curiosity piqued, had decided to cut in.

With a surge of energy she lunged at him, thrusting the gleaming metal towards his chest. Spectators assembled around the room gasped as the yuvraj narrowly escaped being wounded. Protocol demanded that all competitors bow to the yuvraj before beginning to fight, but this opponent had simply ignored that etiquette. He had also entered the room with a turban secured around his face. Who was this daring man?

Shivendra wondered at the audacity of this strange opponent, excitement thrilling through him.

He had spent the last few hours getting bored out of his wits; none of the swordsmen had lasted longer than a few minutes. He had been forced to sit and watch because none had succeeded in overcoming his army officials. Finally, Manvendra had insisted on fighting some of the opponents 'to stretch his legs a little bit', but clearly there was nobody worthy of challenging him in this gathering today. He had been both amused and irritated when a man of such a slight build had vanquished his best soldiers with such ease. Clearly, they were out of practice, it couldn't possibly take him more than a few minutes to defeat his challenger, that is if he lasted that long.

Confidently, he dashed towards his opponent, briefly throwing him; and then stepped backwards, his body already primed for the next attack. For the next few minutes, he found himself supremely matched and even confronted in a sport he thought he had mastered. Both swordsmen charged at each other with unyielding belligerence, as each tried to gain supremacy by outfoxing the other. In their duel, they forgot all about the other spectators, who were now watching intently as they parried on.

Even as the nameless opponent moved away, Shivendra was studying his opponent, trying to predict his next move, but failing. His nameless, faceless adversary changed his line of attack with every move. What he lacked in strength, he made up with his agility and skill. The man fought with the speed and intensity of a seasoned soldier. The man might be small in build, but he was gallant and courageous, fighting with a zeal that was remarkable in itself.

Shivendra could feel the sweat drenching his angrakha as the potency of the fight intensified. It wasn't everyday that the yuvraj came across expertise coupled with such valour. He was as captivated as he was affronted.

Finally, curiosity got the better of him, and, determined to end the duel, Shivendra implemented a faultless dive that ripped the side of his opponent's turban from the left, where it had been secured. Any closer and it would have been his ear.

It was time for his challenger to reveal his identity.

The turban fell to the floor, so skilful had been the cut that had severed it from its bearer's head. The audience gasped.

Shivendra stared in disbelief as a pile of ebony curls tumbled down to the waist of an opponent he at once recognized. He stood spellbound, as he saw, again, Nandini.

He was studying her intently, smiling infuriatingly, as if he was stripping her naked in his mind. Nandini watched disbelief flash briefly across his striking features as he established her identity.

Taking advantage of his reaction, Nandini lunged forward to throw his sword out of his hand, but his grip was too strong, and, as if by reflex, he outmanoeuvred her action by stepping back two paces and slipping the sword from her hands as if it were a toy. His imperial air intimated his authority here, and Nandini gave up her attempts to spar. She was panting from her exertions. His dark eyes glinted dangerously as he studied her face. Nandini's cheeks flushed even further.

Worse, as one of his hands reached out casually

to brush a curl of damp hair away from her flushed cheeks, Nandini could feel tremors running down her spine. He was so close she could feel the heat of his body.

She felt something treacherous and unfamiliar flickering deep within her. A hot flush crept up, inflaming her face. Praying that he couldn't hear the tremor in her voice, she complimented him. 'You fought well, Shivendra, congratulations!'

Her words provoked a sharp intake of breath from the man standing in front of her. 'Give her the mohurs,' he commanded one soldier standing nearby.

'But, Yuvraj, women are not allowed to fight...' Manvendra came forward, but stopped when he saw the look in Shivendra's eyes.

'If she has reached this far, she deserves the mohurs,' Shivendra declared, to the surprise of everyone present.

Nandini was stunned. Was this the arrogant yuvraj allowing a woman to win this coveted prize, one which she had heard he should have won, to prove to the old ministers that his status was deserved? She looked at him, not sure she had heard him right.

Then she gave a tiny shrug, some of her defiance returning. 'I do not accept charity, Yuvraj. Give this to one of your many women. I will not touch something that is not rightfully mine.'

Shivendra tore his gaze from her with difficulty, the sudden tightening of his body reminding him of the power she held over him. This slip of a girl. No, this woman, this woman whom he had to have.

'Consider it compensation, I could have hurt you,'

he said softly, his eyes caressing her exquisite face.

'But you did not, and even if you had managed to kill me, I wouldn't have deserved those mohurs any more than I do now.' Her stare was unfaltering.

It wasn't an answer he'd anticipated. 'And why would a young woman like you want to endanger her life between so many opponents?'

'I think I have just proved I am more than capable of taking care of myself, Yuvraj.' Her tone suggested that she considered the answer obvious.

'By fighting with my best soldiers?' he asked, raising one eyebrow challengingly.

'Absolutely, I mean of course not, it was just a game, a game which I almost won.'

'A game that you did win by defeating the best soldiers of the kingdom. I present you with a sum of a thousand mohurs for your bravery; it is yours. Now take it.'

Startled by his autocratic tone, Nandini opened her mouth to refuse, but he closed long, strong fingers around her wrist and took her forcibly towards the centre of the room, where he handed her the mohurs. Nandini acknowledged her thanks, and turned around and walked out of the hall. The man she most despised, yet was most attracted to, had been just and dignified today. It was all very confusing.

CHAPTER SIX

AMIDST THE GOLD OF the gritty earth and crimson-drenched skies, women, dressed in glittering poshaaks dazzling with mirrors and precious stones, giggled and chatted. Their costumes added colour to the otherwise stark, monochrome landscape and the monotonous sunny sky.

Nandini glanced up at the imposing entrance of the kuldevi temple. The heavy iron double doors leading into the royal temple had been opened to reveal a magnificent, amber-hued sandstone temple rising from the heart of the Thar desert like a golden mirage. The sun's rays flirted with the yellow sandstone of the temple, redressing it in a rich, honey-yellow. Vibrant marigold flowers lined the shallow steps that led to the grand entrance hall of the temple, with its soaring marbled pillars elaborately sculpted with images of goddesses.

Further south, on an elevated stone surface, a goat was being forced to eat dried fruits and milk, which she repeatedly turned away from as if she could predict her impending sacrifice. From the central yard, a kaleidoscope of bright reds, fiery yellows, lively greens and brilliant oranges, highlighted by a lavish use of sparkling gold and silver zari and gota dazzled back at her, along with the sound of raised voices intermingled with the steady beats of shehnais and drums. It was the eighth day of Navratri, and the Ashtami puja had just begun. The people of Jaigarh celebrated Navratri by offering the kuldevi a goat as sacrifice; often especially rearing the goat in family backyards for the ritual offering, as their ancestors had done before them. People eagerly waited for Shivendra to behead the beast with one blow of the sword, as was considered auspicious. She knew how the little creature felt, Nandini thought wryly.

Devika prodded her cousin upstairs to the sandstone balcony especially reserved for noblewomen, where several other familiar faces had already started lining the archways. Impressive pillars and tall arcades ran from one end of the wall to the other, and both girls slipped into the first empty space they could find. Nandini turned sideways to fit behind one of the thick posts, and then peered around it to watch tradition being replayed yet again. She could see people everywhere. Talking, rejoicing, drinking madira, that potent local brew, shouting and cheering for the yuvraj to make an entrance.

She spotted the portly priest first, dressed elaborately today, in a saffron silk dhoti and kurta, a heavy chain of gold and coloured gems looping his shoulders. He stood near the bleating goat, chanting spells and sprinkling holy water on it at regular intervals.

And then she saw him. The world stopped.

The laughing, prattling crowds were forgotten as the

Yuvraj of Jaigarh came into full view of the public. He was just so handsome. Dark and powerful and perfect in his formal attire. Even though she had seen him just a few days ago, she could feel her stomach fluttering. Now amongst his people he stood, erect and proud. He looked like he was used to giving orders that were instantly obeyed. Yet he had been so noble in the way he had handled the outcome of the duel in his durbar hall. She couldn't help warming to him a little.

Slowly, as if for a private audience, he loosened the silk that covered his broad shoulders to reveal an alluring breadth of muscular, bronzed chest, glistening with sweat.

She studied his naked strapping shoulders, broad chest, and narrow hips, and her gaze drifted to his rugged features. Dressed in a crimson dhoti, lined with gold thread, he exuded power, raw sensuality. But who was she to him?

All of a sudden, he raised his eyes and seemed to look up, unswervingly, at her. Nandini froze, her knees almost caving in as she forced herself to hold his gaze.

He couldn't possibly spot her in this kaleidoscope of colour. But his eyes drilled into hers, leaving her completely exposed. She tried to move back into the shadows. But he had succeeded; she felt as if she had been caught in her game of spying on him.

The priest whispered something into Shivendra's ears, and the prince was forced to turn away as Nandini breathed a sigh of relief.

This was the first time Nandini was witnessing a sacrifice; and even though her cousin had assured her that she would enjoy it, she had her doubts. The altar consisted of a large stone with a flagstone on top, placed next to the sacred fire burning in the middle of the elevated surface. The priest began to chant hymns from the Rig Veda as he performed a ritual cleansing of hands with water poured from a sacrificial bowl. Then he sprinkled the goat with yet more water, so that it would shake it off, as a sign of the kuldevi's presence and willingness to receive the sacrifice. Nandini watched the ritual she had just read about take place in front of her eyes in wonder. While the chanting priest sang hymns and swayed juniper branches in the fire, swinging them to and fro, Shivendra appeared from the enclosure that housed the deity of the kuldevi and raised the gleaming blade of the sword, bringing it down with all his force and severing the goat's head with one impressive stroke.

Nandini stood there, too horrified to move as blood gushed out of the beast's twisting torso. She covered her face with her hands, unable to bear the gruesome sight the public seemed to so enjoy. She slipped out, hot tears staining her cheeks and blurring her vision as she made her way down the stairs through crowded arches and groups of women. The scene below was chaotic, people were caught up in rejoicing, dancing around as the carcass of the animal was being dragged away to be cooked in the holy fire so it could be distributed as holy food to the community.

Nandini reached the lowest floor of the temple and promptly realized she was the lone woman in the mardana. So caught up in emotion, she had forgotten to go down from the back entrance.

Lakshya Singh spotted her first, striding towards her with a bottle of liquor in his hand, 'Is my destiny finally smiling at me? Nandini, beautiful Nandini with the infamous viper-like tongue...' He reached out to caress her face, but she turned away in disgust.

'What will you do today? There is nothing to douse me with today, so let me make it easier for you. Shall I drench you with alcohol to make you all the more intoxicating, or would you like to serve me with those porcelain hands?' he said insolently, proffering a bottle of country-made liquor.

'Lakshya, you are drunk, stay away from me! Don't create a scene and let me pass.' Nandini pleaded with him, realizing she had caught the attention of the other men present. They turned to inspect her with bloodshot eyes.

'Pass where? The corridor is full of drunken men; wouldn't you rather entertain me than them? You must miss me. Don't they say "absence makes the heart grow fonder"?' He took a step closer and Nandini could feel his drunken breath on her cheek.

'They also say that familiarity breeds contempt.' Shivendra walked over calmly, standing behind her. 'If you say one more word, Lakshya Singh, I promise you will not live to see the sun set tonight. Now, apologize for your behaviour,' Shivendra commanded.

Lakshya looked like he had been hit by a camel

cart. He muttered something beneath his breath, and bowing low to the yuvraj, disappeared into the recesses of the corridor. To Nandini's horror, however, she could see other men filtering into the passageway. There was going to be a big scene.

As if sensing her apprehension, Shivendra pulled her towards the entrance. His arms were powerful, annoyingly comforting, warm against her cool skin.

They walked through a maze of corridors and rooms in silence; nobody gave them a second look. She couldn't help but be conscious of him as he towered beside her. Be careful, she told herself. He has his designs, and you are just a pawn.

But she found herself following him, into unfamiliar territory. She kept pace as they traced their steps down the narrow corridors, past lines of people merrymaking in the carved stone mazes, before stepping to blend into a horde of peasants assembled in the temple courtyard. Shivendra kept her close at his side.

Nandini felt herself being pushed into one of the narrow corridors of the temple haveli. She staggered, and the yuvraj steadied her by grasping her waist with his strong arm. The throng pushed against them and his grasp tightened, pulling her even closer. She struggled in vain to keep some distance between them, but there was no room for her to escape. The room was thronged with elegantly dressed women who were preparing to leave; and men for whom the festivities had just begun.

She fell against his hard, sinewy body and gasped

at the extent of his desire. A multitude of sensations assaulted her senses; the feel of her breasts crushed against the might of his chest, the warmth of his thigh pressing against her curves. His fingers lightly grazed her spine and Nandini suddenly found it difficult to breathe. A plump, middle-aged woman bumped into her, pushing the couple yet closer, as she rushed past them to catch up with her daughters-in law. She landed against Shivendra just as he closed his arms around her.

Shivendra was aware of the conflict going on in Nandini's mind; he sensed the myriad of emotions going through her head—her anxiety, the desire that her bashful demeanour did nothing to hide, and her apprehension at a situation that had formed entirely out of circumstance. Shivendra had also felt her undeniably womanly form.

His hands skimmed the length of her back, locking in an embrace that trapped her against him. He wasn't about to let this opportunity go. After all, how often could he hope to have fiery Nandini willingly pressed against him?

She looked up, and they stared into each other's eyes. Suddenly, it wasn't about pride or dignity or who won, any more. They could sense the electrifying magnetism between them, attracting them to each other with overwhelming force.

For a split second, Shivendra felt his heart miss a beat; she was enchanting. Her saffron poshaak, lined with rich emerald brocade, fluttered in the morning breeze, her curvaceous body straining against it. Curls tumbled down from her head, escaping the careless plait restraining her locks. In the bright sunlight, her eyes were hazel with tiny specks of gold—a gold more intense than the earrings that adorned her ears. Her flawless ivory skin was even more remarkable against those sensuous, full, rose lips.

Shivendra was seized with an urge to taste them again. Swiftly, he bent down, covering her face with his.

She had known this moment would come, had dreamt about it a thousand times, had wished on shooting stars for it, but still she was not prepared for the somersaults in her stomach when his lips finally touched hers.

He lifted his head up abruptly and caressed the side of her face. She almost moaned out for him not to stop and blinked helplessly, her wide, wondering eyes looking into his. His face was an unreadable mask; only the magnitude of his desire was an indication that he had been affected at all by their kiss.

Her eyes, usually so full of fire, were now soft with trepidation and yearning. 'Shivendra...' she sighed. He felt her sultry voice embrace him, caress his being, obscuring his senses and inviting him to plunder her sweetness. She felt the quickening of his breath, and felt his chest move beneath her palm before he swooped down again to claim her lips.

'Nandini,' he groaned her name, as she stood there, winding her arms around his neck unwittingly. For even in all her dreams, she had never anticipated such raw desire, such passion that overthrew judgement. His fervour terrified her, thrilled her; it stirred in her feelings that she thought didn't exist; stirred an eagerness matching his own.

Nandini learnt the influence of her own desire with each stroke of the impatient hands that caressed her generous breasts and her flat stomach. She had completely abandoned herself to the longing he aroused in her; all rational reasoning was replaced by a hunger so intense that she could not refuse him. Instead, she found herself clinging to him as she passionately moulded herself into him, giving back with a matched ferocity.

'Nandini, Nandini, where are you?' Devika's voice shrilled into the room. Shivendra withdrew his head, staring down at the eyelashes feathering her tinted cheeks. Abruptly, he distanced himself from her even though his hands ached to be buried in the silk of her hair; his lips, to be intoxicated by the sweetness of her mouth. Her lips, swollen and bruised, were testimony to their passion, and her hair had come undone, spilling down her back. Her cheeks were flushed and she swallowed.

'I...I must go,' she mumbled, turning around to join her cousin.

'Wait, when do I see you again?' Shivendra implored.

'I...I don't know, Shivendra. Devika will be here any minute. I must leave,' she pleaded.

'Only if you promise to see me later this evening. I will wait for you at my hunting lodge.'

She nodded. Then, without having the courage to cast more than a passing glance at his striking face, imprinted so deeply in her memory, she turned around and fled down the corridor towards Devika.

'Nandini, where have you been? I have been searching everywhere for you,' Devika said. 'Are you all right? What happened to your hair?' she asked in concern.

'Oh, nothing, I got lost and my plait came undone. Let's hurry back home, Bua hukum will be getting worried,' Nandini said with an enthusiasm that failed to reach her eyes.

'You don't look well; in fact you positively look feverish. I hope you are not coming down with something. I will ask the maid to apply ice packs to your forehead. It's definitely the sun; wait till the sandstorms start, then you will be in no condition to go anywhere.' Devika babbled on, but Nandini's mind was far away.

'Are you even listening to me, Nandini?'

'What? I am sorry, what did you say?'

'I have no idea which world you live in these days—you wake up at dawn to go to the temple; you talk to yourself; you eat half a dozen parathas and even worse, you don't put on any weight; and you get lost in a temple of all places, a temple!' Devika repeated with mock exasperation. Nandini was forced to placate her cousin with weak excuses, knowing she wasn't satisfied. She was in no state to explain.

The two women reached the haveli, washed their feet with scented rose water, and entered the main courtyard. Mogra flowers and unlit candles edged the central courtyard and the corridors in preparation for the Navratri festival. Nandini paused to fold her hands at the temple occupying a corner of the courtyard. The quiet of the hallway was broken by a burst of boisterous female laughter drifting down the stairs from a section of her aunt's chambers, where she usually liked to collect with her friends for chit-chat. 'Ma hukum and her friends seem to be in the middle of a particularly interesting gossip session today,' Devika muttered.

'I think she mentioned some merchants from Varanasi and Jaipur were coming over with wares to sell,' Nandini said.

'Jaipur and Varanasi? Why didn't you mention this earlier? Ooh, I am itching to buy some silk slippers to match my tissue poshaak. And gold threads beaded with semi-precious stones to thread my plait with. Now hurry, Nandini, before Ma hukum picks up another one of those hideous pink outfits.'

Nandini tried her best to smile and join in the enthusiasm.

'Come girls, you have come at the right time. Babulalji has some exquisitely embroidered silk slippers to match your poshaaks, choose what you like.' Shreyas Kanwar sat in the middle of the living room with two of her friends, who were frantically trying to squeeze their rather large feet into the dainty slippers.

'Do you think the canary yellow silk brings out my colour more than the hot pink tissue?' Ratan Kanwar, her aunt's dearest friend, asked, holding up both pieces to her oak-coloured skin.

'Hmm, I think the yellow is a better bet, it is so...striking against your complexion,' Devika said, tongue in cheek.

'How was the Navratri puja, Nandini, did you enjoy yourself?' her aunt asked her, when they had settled down between the bolts of fabrics and slippers.

'Oh, it was wonderful, Ma hukum. Yuvraj Shivendra sacrificed the goat, cutting his head off in a single blow. It means we will be blessed with prosperity and luck, right Ma hukum?' Devika responded.

'Yes, my dear. The sacrifice will please the Devi and she will grant us rain, prosperity and luck. Hadn't Yuvraj Shivendra organized a duel some time back? What happened to that?'

'I hear no one managed to reach the final round; anyway everything that happens in the palace stays in the palace. They guard their secrets very carefully I hear,' Ratan Kanwar piped in. 'However, I did hear that the maharaja will be announcing the yuvraj's wedding when he gets back from Jaisalmer after the monsoon. Don't tell anybody, it's a closely guarded secret, but my maid's sister-in-law just got married to a royal guard and he told her that the yuvraj has agreed to marry the Princess of Mewar—the proclamation can take place any time.'

Nandini sat still, as silent as stone. The very man she had locked lips with but a few minutes ago.

'But these rumours have been floating around for a while now, Ratan,' Shreyas reminded her friend. 'Yes, I am aware of that fact, but apparently the yuvraj is sick of sowing his wild oats and he wants to settle down with a docile, well-bred woman from a powerful kingdom, so the princess fits the bill. Shreyas, I am only getting worried about how much work I have to do. This year's most sought-after invitation must surely be that of Shivendra and the Princess of Mewar, and we can't be seen repeating anything, so there are new poshaaks to be bought, matching jewellery to be ordered, and then we have the added responsibility of dressing up the girls.'

'You are right, Ratan. Rajshree Baisa will definitely try to outdo us all by ordering chiffon from France and satin from Austria to be shipped specially for her poshaak, but this time I shall place orders for a few lengths myself.'

Nandini knew she was going to faint, or else be sick right here in the courtyard, between the silks and the brocades spread out in front of her. In front of everyone, all the women sitting there gossiping and discussing what was being hailed as the wedding of the year, of the man who should have been hers. Her lover, she corrected herself. That was all he saw himself as, and she was nothing to him but his mistress.

'Oh, that sounds wonderful. I think I will place orders for a few bolts of fabric myself. How she loves to show off those dreary daughters of hers, pity they are so dark. Shreyas, at such a big event, I am sure you will find suitors for both your daughter and your niece,' Ratan said, picking up a moon-shaped earring with pearls dangling from the bottom.

'Oh, yes! All the who's who of the Rajput society will be present there. Nobody will want to miss

Shivendra's marital alliance; he is, after all, the biggest catch of the marriage market. Nandini, do you like the rose pink lehenga? It looks lovely against your skin.'

Nandini could feel her world spiralling out of control. She fixed her stare upon her golden silk slippers, hearing no one, sensing nothing. The sun's rays streamed in through the multicoloured stained-glass windows in vibrant shades of the rainbow; the fragrance from the mogra and the lilies decorated around the haveli assaulted her nostrils; she found her throat dry, and no amount of water could quench her thirst.

'Nandini, did you hear me? Do you like the pink lehenga?'

'I am sorry, Bua hukum, I am not feeling too well. I think I shall go and lie down for a while.'

'Oh, you poor child, I thought you looked feverish. Yes, go to your chamber and try getting some sleep. I will send the maid with ice packs and some herbs to ease the discomfort.' Her aunt called out for the maid as Nandini left the room.

She was so naive, she thought, humiliated. Shivendra's potent attraction for women was already a topic for much scintillating gossip; hadn't she learnt anything from it?

He had probably decided to wed the princess long ago; this would link one of Rajputana's oldest families to his own. It held much more weight than some poor girl's emotions. What did she expect? That he would marry her? The divide between the aristocracy and the rest was wider than the ocean. They could have no future together.

Shivendra didn't love; he lusted for her. She could wager he would treat her as callously as he had treated several others before her. And yet his decision to marry the princess was understandable—after all he had responsibilities towards his state which surpassed any personal relationship. The Mughals wouldn't attack Jaigarh knowing it had Mewar's strength behind it; the members of the aristocracy would be more accepting of a princess rather than an impoverished zamindar's daughter. She would be welcomed to society, and would blend right into the codes set by the privileged. Nandini knew she had to find the strength to forget all about the past and escape this situation before she had her heart broken.

Shivendra paced in his palace, glowering yet exhilarated. He had not planned to kiss Nandini but he was glad he did; that one kiss had divulged so much, assuring him of her attraction. Nandini had gotten under his skin; she invaded his every breathing moment, every thought, and every memory, in a way he had thought was impossible. Her reserved uncertainty had been transformed into unreserved passion, enthralling him wholly. He found himself hardening, thinking of the imprint of her abundant form against his body. Their kisses had been explosive; he remembered how Nandini became breathless with growing excitement, her body on fire as his mouth commandeered hers with bruising passion. He could tell she was attracted to him, she wanted him just as much as he wanted her, and yet, she had failed to meet him at the hunting lodge.

He had even sent a messenger to summon her, but all he received was a dismissive and brittle message thanking him for taking care of her on Navratri. It had been three long days now, three achingly long days since he had kissed her. Each minute seemed to shuffle past, making him feel strangely agitated and edgy. Did that angelic face and mesmerizing aura of innocence hide something deeper?

He had no idea what to make of the feisty Nandini with her flashing eyes and pouting mouth. He could barely keep his hands off her. And what was more, she intrigued him. He found himself admiring her bearing, her dignity, her fire; what would it be like to be with a woman like her? He had never known such spirit.

Was she holding him at bay deliberately? Whatever the reason, he needed answers. His soldier had informed him she went to the temple every day and that was where he would get his answers from.

The sky beyond the temple silhouette was heavy with the threat of an impending sandstorm, the arid earth was parched for moisture but the monsoons were still a month away. The temple pandit had warned that there had been torrential sandstorms farther north and they were likely to blow south, towards Jaigarh, but Thakurani Shreyas had laughed and told him she had lived through worse.

The sky was getting darker and greyer, almost as if it were reflecting the state of Nandini's mood. Her aunt had insisted on accompanying her to the temple today, and she busied herself singing hymns while Nandini wandered outside the temple. There was no sign of life outside the usually bustling temple, and she sat by a lily pond in the patch of green that was the temple garden, waiting for her aunt to finish her prayers so she could accompany her back.

Riding into the garden, a tall, masked stranger came to a sudden halt where she sat. Grasping his horse's mane, he jabbed his boot heels firmly into his mount's sides and hoisted himself down to Nandini's height. The horse reared as Shivendra removed his black turban, combing a hand through his coal black hair.

'I thought I would find you here.' Shivendra's eyes were diamond hard. 'Why haven't you replied to my messages or met me? And what was the meaning of that careless note thanking me for my care?' he asked, searching her features. The chill of the early morning air pierced her skin as shivers went down her spine. She had expected him to give up on her as a lost cause, not chase her in full sight of her aunt.

'I don't owe you anything, Shivendra,' she said. 'Not even an explanation.' She stood up, tossed her head back, and glared unflinchingly into his cynical eyes. She would offer him no explanation.

He picked up her hand and brushed his lips over her pulse, his midnight-dark gaze holding hers. 'Yes, you do. I know you are attracted to me, but what will it cost me?' His dark eyes challenged hers.

Nandini snatched back her hand, looking at him

angrily. 'Believe me Shivendra, if I had a price, you couldn't afford me.'

Shivendra paused for a moment, a muscle tensing in his jaw. 'Do you like men chasing you, Nandini? Do you like playing the tease?' he taunted.

She arched her eyebrows at him. 'Maybe I do; maybe I just enjoy playing the games you so love playing; maybe I just decided you weren't a good enough kisser; or maybe I found someone richer than you to seduce.' She gave him a flinty look and moved past him, her heart hammering against her ribcage.

His features went tight with anger. 'Be very careful of what you say, Nandini. I will not be responsible for my actions if you anger me,' he said savagely. 'I just want to know why you didn't answer my messages—give me a reason, for God's sake!'

He did not move, repeating his question as his horse first reared and then pranced about as he brought it easily under control. His question was met with a challenging gaze. The audacity of this man to ask her for an explanation! Just who did he think he was? He obviously thought she was someone of no significance, to be used and thrown like a garland when he had tired of her fragrance.

She was not the one marrying some Prince of Mewar or Marwar or whatever godforsaken kingdom to further her connections; not to boast, but she could have been married to the Nawab of Muzaffarpur by now, if she hadn't bluntly refused to be the third wife of a sixty-year-old pot-bellied nawab. For all he knew, this princess of his would probably smell like garlic and snore in bed, and might weigh as much as Mirchi, her pet camel.

'I am not attracted to you,' she said, glaring at him defiantly, praying he could not detect the tremor in her voice as she delivered this blatant lie.

Her cheeks grew hot as her brain filled with images of him kissing her, which she quickly brushed aside. She knew his desire for her was a purely physical thing.

When his eyes came back to her, they had a brittle edge to them that warned her she had taken things a little too far. 'That is hard to believe, given your enthusiasm—a fact I would love to prove again.' His mouth tilted mockingly. 'If you are not going to tell me, I will just have to make you, won't I?' Shivendra caught hold of his horse by its mane and hoisted himself back on the beast, glaring down at Nandini from an elevation.

'You can do as you please but please excuse me. I can spot my aunt climbing down the temple stairs.' Nandini stood her ground as she brushed past the raging yuvraj, her breath catching in her throat.

He came slowly towards her, without warning, ominous and magnificent, and when he was close enough, he leaned down from the saddle, grasped her by the waist with powerful hands and lifted her up effortlessly. Strong arms closed around her from behind, lifting her off her feet. Nandini let out a cry, in equal measure of fury and fear.

'Shivendra, put me down! Now!' she screamed. She could see her aunt hurrying towards them, the silver thali and the prayer flowers abandoned on the temple steps. There were other women joining her, their voices raised in shrill cries of help.

It was the last thing she remembered before she was borne away. Nandini screamed again, but he just held her body captive against his. Her odhna had fallen back and her silken hair was in his face. Trying not to react to the fullness of her breasts pressed closely against his forearm, he rode westward, to the chattris of his forefathers. There was no sign of any habitation this side of the horizon and a storm was gathering, but the fear of the impending sandstorm was the farthest thing on her mind. Her immediate concern was the reaction this episode would evoke from her aunt. She was sure to tell her father and he would definitely worry for her, at the risk of his own health.

Nandini was tired, tired of thinking of consequences and what ifs. For now, she closed her eyes and tilted her face backwards, losing herself in Shivendra's strong arms.

CHAPTER SEVEN

SHREYAS KANWAR, THE THAKURANI of Trilok watched in disbelief as her niece was snatched up by the incorrigible Prince of Jaigarh. She had heard stories of his wild ways, but this time he had gone too far. Her disbelief gave way to hysterical shrieking, which brought the other women crowding around her. Shreyas had, by then, burst into a torrent of tears, hurling profanities at the rogue yuvraj who had kidnapped her fragile-as-a-flower niece.

'Oh, my innocent little child, she is more than a daughter to me!' she shrieked. 'Anything could happen to her!' Of course, by now she had begun to think about what might be gained from the situation.

'Tsk, tsk, What has the world come to? I hope the poor child is all right,' Ratan Kanwar, the city's most notorious gossip, sympathized, thrilled by the scandalous story she would have to report to the rest of the kingdom.

'At least she didn't get abducted by someone fat and old, Ratan Kanwar. This is all very exciting, just like storybook romances,' sighed Bhubaneshwari Kumari, a dreamy expression in her eyes. Bhubaneshwari, barely sixteen, was the youngest daughter-in-law of an affluent thikana; today she was clad head to toe in bright green, with a kilo or two of ornaments hanging on her frame, from every lobe and ligament. Noticing the older women's expressions, she affected a concerned look, not quite succeeding.

'Yuvraj Shivendra would never harm Nandini; I am sure this is just a misunderstanding,' she consoled Shreyas, lamely.

'A misunderstanding?' the thakurani spat out, having recovered sufficiently to give a choked scream of outrage. 'You call this a misunderstanding? The yuvraj has just abducted my niece and you think we're going to clear this up? Who do you think will marry her now?'

'I...didn't mean that, I mean of course it's not a matter to be taken lightly,' Bhubaneshwari said in her sweetest voice, offering the older woman some water from her thali.

Shreyas sipped the holy water to hide her annoyance at the woman's assumption. 'Yuvraj Shivendra will have to pay for this,' she said. Suddenly business-like, Shreyas announced, 'If he as much as touches my niece, he will have to marry her.'

Ratan clasped a bejewelled hand to her ample bosom. 'You will be related to royalty, Shreyas! This has certainly worked out wonderfully for you,' she said in awe.

Shreyas gave her a withering look. 'As if I would wish such a thing on myself. Now, I must leave before my niece returns uncompromised. I shall have to meet the maharani and enlighten her about her son's activities.'

The land returned to its obdurately stark character after the sandstorm—parched, monotonous, the same for miles as far as the eye could see in any direction. Nandini had unwillingly fallen asleep in her captor's arms, exhausted from the day's exertions. Shivendra surveyed the dark skies with his expert gaze, his years of experience telling him that these clouds would pass them by to drift further west, towards the Arabian Sea. Even though this section of the desert had been worn out by a sandstorm recently, his fine-tuned senses told him there was nothing to worry about now; he rode away, further into the desert, cantering over the sand glistening like gold.

Tenderly, he looked down at the sleeping woman in his arms and realized he wanted nothing more. He had fooled himself long enough, thinking she was another object of his lust, but he now knew that it was her character and fortitude that he was falling for, just as much as her beauty. Now it was time to make amends. She would attack him fiercely for his bold kidnapping, he knew, but she would be convinced by his feelings for her—and, he hoped, of her own feelings for him, which he, fool as he might be, thought he had sensed in her kisses.

He would take her to the old shikar badi, the palatial lodge that his forefathers had built to commemorate their victory over other feuding warlords, and had subsequently turned into a hunting lodge, centuries ago. They would return at nightfall after he had asked her to marry him. For marry her he would, he was determined.

He raised his head to determine the distance to the lodge, and glimpsed its outline, rising out of the golden sea of the great Thar desert. The two rode over parched land and the endless plains till they finally reached the lodge.

Nandini woke with a groggy head, in a room full of inlaid marble, mirrors, turquoise, and hand-carved sandstone pillars. Clutching her forehead, she looked down at the Persian carpets that had long ago been left to disintegrate in obscurity, at the pearl-white pigeons fluttering in the room, at the exquisitely crafted balcony that looked out to the green of an oasis. Where was she? Had she died and perhaps gone to heaven, she thought out aloud, her gaze transfixed on the beauty that she beheld, forgetting, for a minute, how she had been brought here. And then she spotted Shivendra, feeding his stallion freshly cut grass from the oasis opposite. It took a moment for it all to come flooding back and fury surged through her.

'Yuvraj Shivendra, I hope you are happy now,' she said, storming out and raising her voice above the sound of the neighing horse. 'This one reckless act will have my aunt up in arms and my father worrying himself to death. You are the most irresponsible human being I have ever met, and the most arrogant, obnoxious, insufferable, condescending, arrogant...' She bombarded him with insults, not giving him a chance to open his mouth.

'I think you said arrogant twice,' Shivendra observed, mouth twitching.

'I know!' she screamed. 'And please don't interrupt me!'

'You mean I shouldn't interrupt you while you are hurling a string of abuses at me?' he asked, with a devilishly unsettling grin.

Nandini ignored him. 'As I was saying, you deserve to be locked up in a dungeon, or fed to the lions, or left alone between a Mughal army and...or thrown into the deep seas, banished to a distant land,' she finished with flourish.

'I had no idea that behind that pretty little face of yours was a mind with such devious designs,' the prince replied calmly.

'There's a lot more that you don't know about me, Yuvraj, and I would prefer to keep it that way,' Nandini responded haughtily.

'Like the way you curled up around me as a reaction to my kiss? Or the way you kissed me back with those bee-stung lips, so full of promise, your ardour making up for all your inexperience?'

Nandini was unprepared for this. Her eyes lowered to the ground, and despite herself, she felt warmth creeping up her neck. Averting her glance, she composed herself. 'A kiss is just a kiss, Yuvraj, and you, of all people, should know that.'

She dismissed all he had said with a careless movement of her hand. 'As for now, what do you intend to do with me?' she demanded.

Shivendra's eyes had never left her, observing her

intently. 'We will talk about it once you can think calmly,' he informed her coolly. He was determined to make her come to him, to make her admit to what was so clearly a connection between them.

'I am cool, in fact I am so cold I am almost shivering. Now pray enlighten me, what are your intentions?' she asked.

'You will remain here with me until I say so,' he said, ignoring her sarcasm.

'And if I don't?' she challenged.

'Suit yourself. As you can see, there isn't very far you can go,' he pointed out, his gaze skimming the dusty horizon.

'I will scream, I will create a scene, I will...I will...' Nandini stopped mid-sentence, realizing there wasn't anyone to hear her scream or see a scene.

'Be my guest,' he drawled, feigning a yawn as he left her to walk outside.

Nandini was in about as dreadful a frame of mind as it was possible to be in. She abandoned the idea of napping for a while and instead, she began thinking of a possible escape. After a few minutes, she gave up, having surveyed the land, tried to calculate what lay east and west, and further challenged her position. She realized she was alone in a decrepit old lodge, with no servants in attendance and not a soul in sight. She didn't even know where this godforsaken place was. But she had to escape before her aunt sent news of this incident to her father.

All of a sudden, her gaze fell on the marwar grazing on freshly cut grass outside. The oasis was about a metre away. If she needed water, she would have to step into the oasis to collect it from its axis. Her mind began working overtime as she began planning her escape. Patience, she told herself. It was essential that she timed herself to the second, Shivendra was not born yesterday and she needed to convince him.

Shivendra walked into the room a few minutes later, removing the turban protecting his head from the scorching sun. He stood silently in the shadows of the stone structure, admiring the feisty woman sitting on the stone pavement of the balcony, gazing out with a fierce determination at the oasis. She looked like the goddess of fire, her striking features bathed in the glow of the setting sun. What impressed and surprised him simultaneously were the abundance of pride and the intensity of her determination.

He walked towards her and carelessly tossed a small camel leather bag towards her. 'Here is some pickled mutton, you should eat something.'

She cautiously undid the strings of the pouch and picked up a piece of the dried meat. She hadn't eaten anything the entire day, and she relished its spicy, tangy flavour with unveiled delight.

'Can I drink some water, please? My throat is parched,' she said after chewing the meat for a while, in her most polite tone.

Shivendra eyed her suspiciously. 'I will fetch it from the oasis. I won't be a minute,' he said, turning and walking down to the oasis.

Nandini threw the leather pouch down as his steps faded, and scurried towards the unsuspecting marwar. The stallion had been idly pawing at the grass, nibbling bits, but now it lifted its head and pricked up its ears. Nandini knew this would be her only chance. She caught the marwar by its mane, and in a single stroke, mounted herself on its back; she was an accomplished horse rider.

Not used to anyone but Shivendra riding it, the marwar neighed at the intrusion, but Nandini was too skilled for the thoroughbred. The stallion let out a belligerent whinny, protesting agitatedly as she jerked the reins, kicked its shins and rode away. Then the horse swayed slightly to the left, swung ninety degrees to the right, suddenly picking up an unexpected speed, its caramel tail painting the wind behind them.

Rider and horse were locked together in a battle to gain the upper hand, and unfortunately for Nandini, she had no idea which way Jaigarh was. She cursed herself for sleeping through the journey but took solace when she spotted a camp in the far distance. She would ask for directions there. Apparently the horse had the same thought, galloping towards the camp. Too upset to stop at the entrance, it kept running right through the makeshift checkpost at the entrance and into the centre.

Too late Nandini realized that this was probably not a Rajput camp. Rather, it was the evil amir's camp, probably on their way back to Ajmer. There were tents pitched on either side, and a few men sat around a fire cooking their evening meal, while others were busy tying up horses to the posts outside the tent. A few soldiers came running towards them. One of them flashed his mashaal in front of the horse, while the others surrounded them, carrying swords and stubs of sticks. The terrified horse lunged forward and dropped Nandini on the ground, kicking a soldier with his forelegs before galloping back into the darkness.

Her head hurt and her body felt bruised and battered; but Nandini didn't have much time to feel the pain, immediately followed by a perturbing fear of the unknown. Her senses tingled with the realization that she was surrounded by soldiers wearing strange garb, brazenly leering at her. One of them stepped directly behind her, while a pair of them walked menacingly towards both her sides, blocking off all escape routes. A fraction of a second later, she felt a bulky hand fasten over her mouth. Dread overwhelmed her instantly as she tore at the hand and kicked back at her assailant.

But her hands were soon pulled from her face and dragged firmly behind her back. Her odhna fell open so that the wind blew all its chilly force against the finely spun fabric of her lehenga. Nandini's hair came undone and formed a veil around her face, obscuring her vision partially. She tried again to lash out at her assailants but her efforts were all to no avail.

'Wildcat!' an out-of-breath male voice said from behind her, in a tone that welcomed the diversion. 'Though she is a real beauty...'

'The amir will be pleased; she looks like she belongs to an influential Rajput family,' said another.

'Maybe he will give us the leftovers, for all the work we are doing,' a third jested crudely. She could sense him watching her before his hand reached for her left cheek. She waited for his thumb to reach the corner of her lips before she bit into his hand with all her strength. 'Mad bitch, you will be whipped for this!' he screamed in agony, reaching to strike her face.

'What the hell is taking so long, haven't you gotten her wrists bound yet?' another man asked, approaching the scene.

'She is struggling like a lioness, Huzoor,' another voice said. 'There. That should secure her hands.' Nandini screamed in agony as the rope tied around her wrists cut into her flesh, making her fragile skin bleed.

'Stuff something into her mouth. Ruftaq, get me a piece of cloth to bind her mouth with,' the first man said. 'We don't want her to attack the amir, he will definitely feed us to the tigers. These women are all fire—as if riding alone into our camp after sunset was not bad enough, they refuse to submit gracefully either. I hope she is worth the trouble.'

Nandini was not listening to the conversation any more. As they talked, the second man was tying a scarf tightly over her mouth. She stomped her feet and twisted her torso with renewed vigour, but the knot slashing into her skin only cut in deeper, staining the pastel of her lehenga with blotches of red blood. Her captors took her to a dark tent.

Nandini panicked, imagining the fate that awaited her. She had heard of the Mughals' soldiers committing atrocities against Hindu women in the villages. What did they intend to do with her? She hoped and prayed they were only planning to murder her, stab her or burn her. She would rather die than be ravished by these men—the very thought made her stomach churn in revulsion. She just needed to kill herself with honour before they had a chance to kill her. Also, she wondered if there was a chance Shivendra would find her. He may have been as forceful as these men, but she still felt safe with him. But there was no hope of this, she thought gloomily.

The crowd of soldiers approached her before she could try to come up with a plan to escape, bursting into her tent and dragging her out, into a larger tent, to their leader.

'Who is this girl?' a new, authoritative voice asked in annoyance. 'Have you hoodlums nothing better to do than abduct village girls?'

'Huzoor, she rode into our camp. I think she is either a spy or lost in the desert. Her manner and carriage say she is Rajput,' the soldier whispered conspiratorially.

'Remove the scarf,' the man said, staring at the woman before him with renewed interest. 'Quite a beauty, this one—well done!' He rose to come forward towards her and Nandini took an involuntary step backwards, which greatly amused him. 'My sweet little shy pet, there is nothing to fear any more.' He laughed. 'Remove the scarf and leave us alone,' he ordered, his tone suddenly changing.

The scarf removed, Nandini was finally set down on a feather-stuffed divan. For the first time, she raised her eyes to study the man who stood before her. Her captor was a middle-aged man with a long beard and a thinning, almost bald scalp, which he stroked almost fervently. He stepped towards her, lifting her chin with the crook of his thumb.

'Subhaanallah, you are beautiful. You don't look like a spy, but why would somebody as beautiful and young as you be travelling alone without a chaperone?' He smiled leeringly at her. 'Don't wish to speak? I am much used to taming unwilling hussies like you.'

'I am not unwilling, Huzoor, just tired. The bonds hurt my hands and my body aches,' Nandini whispered coyly. If she had any chance of getting away, she needed her bonds to be cut off. She saw her plan succeeding when the amir's face broke into a beaming smile.

'Here, my pet,' her captor said, fumbling with her bonds until he found the knots at her wrists. 'I can't see someone as angelic as you in agony, now, can I?'

Nandini's frenzied struggles gave way to a coy smile. If the amir had known Nandini better, he would have realized that this was the smile she reserved to mislead suitors before she shamed them into defeat.

If she escaped from this man, she had a whole camp of enemies to get past before she could regain her freedom. She prepared herself to die fighting, yet again, smiling wryly when she imagined Shivendra's guilt at having been the cause of her untimely death. 'Serves him right, I suppose,' she thought. She was glad she hadn't lost her sense of humour even in such dire circumstances.

The amir reached out for her hand, smiling, and her half-hearted protests did nothing to stop his advances. Close, but not close enough. He came forward to embrace her and in a flash, she pulled out his sword, twisted it around, and struck him in his thigh.

'Aaahh, the whore!' he screamed. 'Muhammed, Sadamat, Ahmed...where is everybody?'

Nandini ran towards the window, tearing it open and tumbling out into the quiet dark of the night. All sound, except the pulsing of her throbbing heart, was wiped out as she slunk out of the camp, alone. Her lehenga swirled about her legs as she ran faster, careful to avoid the checkpost to her left. Fleeing the glow of lanterns lighting the tents, she raced up a sandy path at the edge of the camp, her long hair tangled and wild. Her face was ashen with terror as she repeatedly glanced over her shoulder, ensuring she was not being followed.

Nandini staggered on, falling to her knees a few times, but quickly jumping back to her feet. The moonlit silver sands glistened before her eyes. The scraggy hills on the horizon seemed an eternity away, the hills that shadowed Jaigarh in their lap.

Her eyes closed for a second and her mind was filled with images of home, of Multan, her doting father, Jaigarh and, unexpectedly, Shivendra. 'He was the first man I really kissed, after all,' she allowed. But there was something more than his brooding good looks; she found herself thinking of his oddly caring ways, the moments in which he seemed to reveal himself as more than a bored playboy. Moments, only moments, she reminded herself as she trudged on. She couldn't tell why he was singling her out, why he had abducted her, though. Perhaps the kingdom had run out of willing courtesans.

She stiffened. Her instincts told her she wasn't alone. Still on the fringes of the camp, she gulped dryly as she saw the shadows of horsemen passing her by. Dropping to the ground and pressing her body into the sand, she moved backwards, out of sight and into the darkness, lying still for what seemed like hours, and fearing desert snakes all the while. But she knew the riders would be back; they would realize she couldn't get far and retrace their steps, scanning the barren landscape till they found her.

And she was right. The riders came back in a downpour of black, their horses kicking up fountains of sand. She ascribed their vigour to the amir's having been insulted, as well as injured, by a Rajput, and wondered when this would end.

Burrowing more deeply into the sand, she waited against the storm of hoof beats, which had grown thunderous. Then they went away; only to leave three soldiers open to her line of vision.

The battle-hardened soldiers wore dark, flowing kurtas and grey turbans over gathered pyjamas. Their impenetrable faces were tanned and leathery from fighting and losing battles under the fierce sun, their lives a testimony to the innumerable people whose lives they had destroyed, whose treasures they had plundered. The soldiers had collected in a semicircle now; they were speaking in Urdu, a language she was familiar with, having grown up in Multan. She stood very still, listening to their heated conversation, which could only be about her whereabouts. From the corner of her eye, she spotted an exit; if she could somehow manage to crawl to the gate, she could hide behind the post till they rode away. She was slinking towards it, crawling on her stomach, when suddenly, she felt an arm around her, yanking her up roughly.

She was pulled against something hard and impenetrable, and found herself facing what seemed like a wall of iron.

Her breasts were now pressed against a masculine chest, which she struggled against wildly for a second, but he reassured her at once. It was Shivendra.

'Shh, you are safe,' he whispered. The relief flowing through her was immediate. The prince wrapped his arms around her, his broad, muscled shoulders bracing her against the cold of the desert.

She did not move, and it was impossible to tell in the darkness if he was looking at her. 'How did you find me?' she questioned, her voice coming out in gasps.

'The horse led me to you. I was waiting for darkness to infiltrate the camp but you acted sooner than I had planned.' He looked at her, with eyes that were dark in the shadows, yet she could see, admiring. 'I followed your escape and joined the group of soldiers as one of them, slowly striking them down one by one,' he said grimly. This was why there had been only three soldiers, Nandini realized, all of a sudden.

Nandini looked at Shivendra in awe: she had placed both their lives in jeopardy, and yet he had saved her. Of course, she reminded herself, they wouldn't be here in the first place if it wasn't for him.

The yuvraj gestured for her to follow him to the marwar, which he silently helped her mount, as he pulled himself up. He held her in place with his arms as they rode back in silence to the hunting lodge.

Back at the lodge, Shivendra offered her water from the camel skin pouch. She drank deep. The water was warm, and flowed smoothly down her parched throat. He busied himself in lighting a fire and Nandini tried to rest her body against a pillar. But she grimaced with pain as her back touched the cool of the stone, her wounds staining it red. Shivendra walked towards her, stopping a few feet in front of her.

'Are you in pain?' he asked her.

She nodded almost imperceptibly.

'I will have to clean your wound, turn around.' It was a command, not a question.

She hesitated and slowly turned around. He regarded her shoulder in silence for a few moments. The blouse had been ripped, and Nandini had several small cuts on her back.

'This might make you cry,' he warned.

'I don't cry in front of strangers,' she said. Her voice was soft, devoid of either the severity or the harshness that he had expected.

He dampened the end of his undone turban and handed it to her. 'Wash your face. Your skin looks sunburnt and grimy.'

The wet cloth was solace, moistening her scorched, dehydrated skin and peeling away layers of dirt and sand. 'Thank you, you're very kind.'

His brows rose. 'Am I? You seem to know me better than I know myself.' He paused. 'Did the amir dare to harm you in any way?' he asked quietly, but with an unmistakable touch of steel in his voice.

'No,' her response was firm. She knew what he meant. 'I didn't give him the chance to.'

His relief was immediate. Looking at Nandini with narrowed eyes, the yuvraj slipped off her tattered blouse, cleaning the wound with a mixture of chalk and slate before applying crushed herbs to it. She winced but bore the pain bravely.

Shivendra stopped himself from reaching out to her. He was not going to offer comfort when she clearly needed none from him; she had demonstrated that she wanted no emotional comfort, or anything for that matter, from him.

Having dressed her wound, Shivendra turned his attention to preparing dinner for the both of them. Expertly, he skinned the wild boar he had set a trap for earlier, preparing it in an age-old recipe for junglee maas, passed down the generations. Maas was made from the meat of a wild animal and was cooked in pure ghee, with salt and red chillies. The simplicity of the dish owed itself to the paucity of fine cooking ingredients available in a hunting campsite.

After cleaning the animal, Shivendra stuffed it with a marinade of chillies, salt, and kanchri, a local herb imparting a distinctive tang to the meat, and barbecued it over a bed of live coals. Traditionally called sula, the meat was known to take on a tangy, smoked taste, as a result of its preparation.

The two settled down to feast on the delicacy and some vegetables.

'Shivendra, if you hadn't rescued me, what would have become of me?' Nandini asked him thoughtfully, in between mouthfuls of meat. The prince started slightly.

'I didn't rescue you, you rescued yourself, I simply helped you escape,' he stated, offering her more water. 'Amir Azam Ali is notorious for selling captives to the slave market or killing them, but I think he had different plans for you.'

Her eyes widened. 'You know him personally?'

'I do not know any of the Mughals. Simply put, I am just acquainted with them, especially on the battlefield. There's a difference,' he said, looking up at her with piercing eyes.

'What will happen when he finds out his men have been slain?' she asked, sipping her water slowly.

'He will keep quiet, if I know him well. It is not like the amir to make his camp a laughingstock by publicizing the fact that a woman killed half a dozen of his best soldiers.' He reassured her, 'I have left no clues—nobody saw me enter or leave.'

Shivendra was aware that if the amir decided to attack, he would need more troops from Ajmer. However, the political conditions in Agra would not permit any troops to be spared for an insignificant kingdom like Jaigarh. Emperor Akbar's son, Salim or Jehangir as he was popularly called, had, during the absence of his father from Agra, pronounced himself emperor and turned rebellious. Akbar had been able to wrest the throne back, but the political situation was highly strained. There was also an unconfirmed story of a tense relationship between the father and son due to Salim's amorous advances on an ordinary dancing girl. The power struggle had left much of Hindustan fragmented, and both Muslim and Hindu rulers had failed to create a common body of laws or institutions. However, Jaigarh had a strong army of its own, and could resist attacks from neighbouring kingdoms and Muslim nobles. Shivendra was sure they would be able to withstand a potential attack.

Nandini abruptly changed the subject, breaking into Shivendra's thoughts. 'Have you forgiven me yet?'

'There is nothing to forgive; it was my fault for forcing you to come here. Tomorrow, I will make amends and take you back to Jaigarh.'

'That is good to know,' Nandini responded slowly, thrown. So the prince had tired of her, at last.

'We have a long journey ahead of us when the sun rises, sleep now,' the yuvraj said, and he turned to walk in the direction of the horse. 'I have made a bed of hay for you next to the fireplace.'

Nandini fell into step beside him. They did not exchange a word. She stood quietly at his shoulder as he checked on the horses, and then lay down on the bed, her body so slight that he half turned his head to make sure she was there.

Shivendra settled in for the night, allowing Nandini her privacy by sitting at an angle and putting out the single mashaal that he had been carrying. He knew the desert like the back of his hand; there was no fear for him, just the familiarity of being, once again, under the star-filled nights of the desert.

Nandini slept as soon as her head touched the bed. Her hair was spread across the makeshift hay bed like a waterfall of gleaming black diamonds. She was exquisite and beautiful, he saw again, but it was the fire rushing through her that he was in love with.

Her chin lifted an inch as she mumbled something in her sleep, her mouth moving sensuously even in her sleep. It was going to be a long night.

He bowed his head over her until he could feel her breath against his hair, and closed his eyes, to fall into a dreamless sleep.

Shivendra swung the crudely made wooden handle of the axe up over his head and savagely slammed it down again, splitting the stump of a tree perfectly down the middle. The sound split across the shimmering sand as noiselessly as an arrow, stirring the squirrels and wild rabbits that fed on the desert flowers blooming near this oasis.

The axe appeared to be an extension of his limb, as man and instrument worked in perfect harmony, smoothly, effortlessly, the sweat flowing down his tanned back the only indication of the effort he was putting in. Shivendra carelessly tossed the bisected halves of the wood to one side, adding them to the already stacked pile of wood lying on the side. He threw down his axe for a minute, stopping only to wipe his body dry with a piece of muslin, and picking up the axe again, began to arrange the wood and chop it with one precise blow of power. Even though he concentrated on this effort wholeheartedly, his thoughts kept wandering, against his better judgement, to the woman sleeping a few metres away.

He was a fool to think she had any feelings for him. She couldn't bear to spend one day alone with him, so desperate was her hatred that she had escaped, preferring death to him. He struck the wood again—more savagely this time, creating a small crater in the land below it.

All of a sudden, he noticed that his sweating body was the centre of someone's intense attention. He could feel Nandini's eyes on his movements. Casually, he wiped the sweat off his brow with the back of his arm, and not bothering to cover his naked torso with the angrakha lying at his feet, turned around to look her straight in the eye.

Embarrassed, Nandini quickly turned her face away. He had caught her looking at his body with what could only be described as lust in her eyes.

Shivendra watched her with satisfaction as her cheeks turned a flaming red, a small ray of hope surging through him—after all, he couldn't possibly be all that repulsive to her if she could look at him like that.

Nandini reluctantly turned her gaze away, even though her eyes longed to caress his form again. She had seen him earlier but he had always been clothed. Now, she had gazed at those golden shoulders moist with glistening sweat, midnight waves curling around his forehead until his hand coarsely combed them back, forming grooves in his hair. The deep gold of his skin was in sharp contrast to the stark white of his pyjamas. Of course, most powerful as always were his relentless black eyes, gleaming dangerously and boldly moving lower, caressing her as they passed over her body.

Nandini found herself struggling to suppress the powerful urge to give in to those magnetic eyes, wicked as she knew them to be.

'Good morning. Did you sleep well?' Shivendra's voice broke into her confused thoughts, his gaze deliberately tracing the lines of her faultless oval face, the sharp angle of her pert, slightly upturned nose, and the succulent curve of her strawberry-red lips. If he had thought her beautiful before, he found her irresistible now.

Nandini sat up, the question somehow having taken her unawares. She pulled the pink odhna towards her and clutched it to her breast. She looked as fresh as a drop of dew, he thought. She also looked somewhat unhappy.

'We have a long journey ahead of us. I suggest you walk down to the oasis and wash up,' he told her.

Her mouth did not slip from its downward arch. 'Are we leaving already?' She spoke her thoughts out aloud and realizing the implication of the statement, tried hurriedly to make amends. 'I mean, it is so serene here, must we leave so early?'

Shivendra watched her with raised eyebrows and suppressed a smile. 'I thought you wanted to leave, you did seem very eager yesterday,' he said casually, as he readied his horse for the journey. 'Anyway, we must prepare to leave soon, before the sun reaches overhead and it gets too hot to ride.'

Nandini couldn't hide her disappointment at his statement, but she silently gathered the folds of her lehenga and, sulkily, walked down to the oasis.

The sun had already begun to scorch the desert as Nandini and Shivendra galloped through the untouched valleys of sand dunes, crossing the magical landscape of arid canyons and gorges. Shivendra tilted his head suddenly, and slowing the horse, he tightened his hold on the reins and steadied the horse while his practised gaze assessed a cloud of sand in the horizon beyond. A group of soldiers rode towards the couple in all their finery. Manvendra, dressed regally in a scarlet turban, reached them first, discreetly turning his face away from Nandini's as he bowed low to Shivendra.

'Khamagini.'

'Khamagini, Manvendra, is all well in the kingdom?' Shivendra asked, in a voice reserved for official concerns, suddenly transforming into the heir of Jaigarh, before Nandini's startled eyes.

'Yes, Hukum, all is well. Your mother, the maharani, has directed us to find your whereabouts and deliver this letter to you,' he responded, taking out a red velvet roll from his waistband that he passed on to Shivendra. 'I have been instructed to wait while you read it and decide on the course of action,' he added, turning his horse around to provide Shivendra with the privacy he needed to read the message. Shivendra cracked open the wax seal and began reading his mother's message.

With the blessings of our kuldevi upon your head, I am sure this letter will find you healthy and safe, my dearest son. By the time this letter will find you, I will be in Jaisalmer with your father, the maharaja. I only write to warn you not to come back to Jaigarh. The unfortunate episode between you and that local girl has been exaggerated into a much bigger affair. As you are aware, she is of noble birth and her 'abduction' (though I can never believe you would abduct anyone) has caused a small scandal in the city. The noblemen have found one more grouse against you, so I beg you to return home only once the matter has cooled. The girl's pushy aunt insists that you marry the commoner to restore her honour but I shall leave that up to you as you are the best judge of the situation.

I have decided to go to Kunihar early. As you are aware, your cousin is to be wedded there next month and the celebrations shall start any time now. I would prefer that you meet us there as well and then we can jointly resolve the matter. I have already asked the maharaja to accompany me and I am happy to inform you, he has complied with my wishes. This means you have time to think the matter over. Whatever you decide, my blessings are always with you but like every mother, I hope you will make the correct decision and not get forced into a situation not to your liking.

Let Jaigarh always be blessed with prosperity and happiness!

Your loving mother

Shivendra read the letter twice before tearing it into shreds. He swung his leg over the saddle and, securing Nandini firmly to him, slid with her to the ground. He left her standing there and walked to where Manvendra stood waiting for his answer.

'How serious is the situation?' he asked his closest friend.

'It will take a moon cycle to die down—people will find something more entertaining and they will forget all about this incident,' Manvendra answered, honestly.

'What about Nandini?' Shivendra asked, taking a minute to turn around and smile reassuringly at the woman standing behind him.

'Her situation will be more delicate; this "incident" has left her honour completely compromised, and no nobleman in Jaigarh will touch her. However, a marital alliance can be arranged outside Jaigarh. The maharani has promised her aunt that she will take care of the wedding expenses and her dowry,' Manvendra informed him.

'That will not be necessary. I have decided to marry her as soon as possible,' Shivendra said, not missing a beat.

Years of careful upbringing didn't prevent Manvendra from showing his shock at this announcement. But he recovered quickly. 'As you please, Hukum, but no priest in Jaigarh will perform the ceremony without the maharaja's blessings, and as you know, if you decide to marry her outside, the people will not have faith in the sanctity of your vows.'

The yuvraj looked at him impassively. Carefully, Manvendra added, 'Forgive my saying this, Hukum, but Nandini's...er...circumstances have been compromised after this abduction—it has branded Nandini wanton and impure for marriage, especially with a prince.'

'I want you to relay to Nandini's aunt that I have decided to claim her hand in full view of the Jaigarh people. With Lord Agni's blessings, we will be bound together in the holy vows of matrimony. Tell her to send a message to her father summoning him to Jaigarh at once.' Shivendra gave his commands coolly and calmly. His father would understand and the kingdom would be silenced.

'Are you sure, Yuvraj?' Manvendra asked one last time.

'This is my duty, Manvendra, I must marry her to calm wagging tongues. As my wife, she will be yuvrani, and receive all the respect that comes with the title.'

Shivendra heard a strangled gasp from behind him. 'But I do not wish to marry you, Yuvraj, not now, not ever—you can keep your palaces and titles, I do not wish to be bound to you.' Nandini stood directly behind them, her eyes flashing fire.

Shivendra turned around to face her squarely. 'I don't remember giving you a choice.' Silence filled the space between them.

'I do have a choice, I am not yours to command, Yuvraj. I don't belong to your kingdom, and you don't have the right to order me around like I am one of your cattle.' She blazed, her eyes dark with belligerence.

'We shall discuss this later, Nandini,' he growled, his eyes glinting dangerously. Nandini hesitated and hung back, still ready to fight him on this later. 'Manvendra, I want you to do as you have been ordered to. Also, tighten the defence line for the next few days while I am away. I entrust the kingdom's safety to your able hands,' he said authoritatively, and with that, Shivendra dismissed Manvendra and strode back to the stationed horse.

Nandini watched Shivendra walking back towards her. Assembling all her might, she turned and faced his ire—with her own. But when she looked at him, she found herself admiring him for the second time in the day; when she looked at his dark hair, she remembered how it had curled near his neck, how silky it had felt between her delicate fingers when he had kissed her senseless. She tried to push the memory of his lips—so firm yet so gentle, coaxing her, teasing her—out of her head. The intensity of his passion had been demanding, his hands had burnt her bare skin, making her tremble in pleasure.

Most of all she struggled to banish all thoughts of her reaction to his kiss—she had been left aching for more, had clung to him with a passionate ferocity and kissed him back, his body had moulded every curve...But she chided herself yet again. Shivendra wasn't marrying her because he loved her, but because he had to perform his duty. She had heard snatches of his conversation with Manvendra and now knew this for a fact. What a fool she had been to think otherwise. Now, she could not let her emotions betray her, even though her heart was fluttering wildly in her breast. She would put up a brave face now, and reject his offer. He had disregarded one trivial detail—it was her acknowledgement and not his offer that made a difference.

She pulled herself together to confront him. As he neared, she realized again just how very tall he truly was. His cream angrakha clung to his muscled torso, outlining shoulders that looked wide enough to carry the world upon them. Her gaze glided down to stop at his hands, hands she had known to be tender when they caressed her. She would convince him, though, that she had felt nothing more than a passing fancy towards him. When she finally looked him in the eye, she expected to meet his fathomless black gaze; but gone was his angry mask. Her skin flushed when he looked back at her with an unanticipated tenderness.

'As you have overheard,' he began, his voice commanding, yet calm, 'I have ordered Manvendra to arrange for our wedding to take place as soon as possible.'

Nandini looked down, hiding the hope in her eyes, willing him to say he loved her, that he was marrying her because he wanted to spend his life with her.

Shivendra exhaled with relief; she wasn't refusing him, at least. 'I know I should have discussed this with you, but it was a decision that I felt I had to make, to right the wrong I have done to you, even though you may feel otherwise.'

Nandini felt her heart twinge. A decision he was forced to make to save her honour, a decision he would grow to regret eventually, she thought to herself. Nandini wanted to believe that he loved her, but it was all too clear that he was only marrying her to restore her honour. She bit her lip hard, deciding this torture had to end.

Unaware of Nandini's inner turmoil, Shivendra continued, 'If there is anything specific that you want in your trousseau, you just have to ask for it. You will move into my palace after we get married, instead of living in the zenana; and the palace zenana will be converted into a section for our children when they come. Do you have something else that you want?'

She would not accept scraps of his pity. With a steely determination in her voice, she took a step forward to face him with the same arrogant confidence that he displayed. Meeting his look evenly, she asked him, 'Do I have a right to voice my opinion about this sudden decision of yours?'

Without waiting for him to reply, she carried on. 'Thank you for your kind offer to restore my honour, but I am not in need of your favours, Yuvraj Shivendra.'

The yuvraj turned to look across the horizon, silently. Nandini gathered up her courage and stepped forward to face him once more. Placing her hands firmly on her hips, she made her final argument. She might as well tell him every reason she wasn't considering marrying him. Except that one.

'I would rather die an old maid than marry you, Yuvraj. From where I come, respect and love are placed above status and duty—I might be poor and people may gossip about me, but I will not marry you to save face!'

His eyes burned into hers. Masking the expression on his face, he asked, 'So, you do not wish to be the next Maharani of Jaigarh because you don't love me?'

She held her ground solidly even if it meant lying to him. 'Well, I can hardly marry someone for whom I feel a mild warmth and nothing more.'

'A mild warmth, is it? I have seen this warmth bubble over with passion, and don't you dare deny the connection between us. Nandini, you know you are lying to yourself.' Shivendra grew endearingly passionate, abandoning all show of restraint. 'Or have you changed your mind and wish to be my *mistress* instead?'

'Have you never heard of pretence? Maybe I am attracted to the man who offers the most?' said Nandini, suspicious of this tempting admission on the yuvraj's part and incensed at his offer. He was bluffing. And she could play along.

She watched his eyes blacken into livid pools of fire. 'You are not a very convincing liar—if you were looking to milk the richest fool, you could have married the Sultan of Muzaffarpur or the Amir of Sarika; and if it is money you want, it is one commodity I have in plenty.' The yuvraj looked outraged, Nandini noticed, somewhat satisfied.

He stepped closer to her and only too late, she realized that they were standing a little too close; she could almost feel his breath on her forehead. An overwhelming attraction pulled her to him, uncontrollably, seeming to draw them closer—desire burnt through her like coals, willing her closer to him.

She felt the familiar surge of passion; she was a puppet in his hands, left at the mercy of the senses he had so expertly aroused each time he drew near her. She had to be strong enough to resist him—to pull away before it was too late.

She took a step back but instead, found herself clasped close to Shivendra. He had felt the raw attraction between them as well, and pulling her to him, he looked down into her limpid eyes. 'You insist on lying to yourself, on believing there is nothing between us, so maybe *I* need to prove just how attracted you are to me, Nandini.'

'Shivendra, don't, please don't!' she said, her eyes filling. Her breasts tightened agonizingly as she struggled to catch her breath. She pushed against his chest, but the struggle only caused him to hold her closer. He wrapped his hands around her waist, trapping her body against his, shocking her with the extent of his desire. Passion and yearning turned her resolve into water; her turbulence turning into longing for him; her breasts rose and fell rapidly; her nipples tightened into tiny rosebuds pressing through the thin fabric she wore.

Shivendra bent down to kiss her lips, his tongue cajoling and teasing the tip of her own tongue—available to him as her lips were still parted, in surprise—before moving back to her mouth. Not until Nandini moaned in protest did he press his lips against hers finally, with abandon.

Pushing his body to mould against hers, his expert mouth moved downwards to leave a trail of kisses from the nape of her neck to the creamy cleavage peeping from her chiffon odhna. Grabbing her odhna, he threw it away, undoing her hair with one hand while the other moved down her curves, pleasuring her skilfully.

Nandini kissed him back, with equal intensity—suddenly she couldn't think, only letting her body lead the way. Her hands passionately roamed the breadth of his back before slipping into the open V of his angrakha, exploring the chest she had only admired from afar. Shivendra opened his eyes, shocked at the intensity of her emotions.

Their eyes met at the same moment as their lips. Tender and enticing one minute, passionate and exacting the other, the yuvraj ravished her mouth. She was sure her legs would give way; that she would fall into the bottomless pit of passion that he aroused; or melt into a puddle at his feet, were it not for his hand holding her against his iron-hard body.

Shivendra heard Nandini beg and moan in ecstasy. She was a novice to the feelings his experienced hands could arouse, albeit an irresistible one. Lost in desire, her eyes half closed, her lips parted, she looked like a goddess. Did she know what an unwitting seductress she was?

It took all his self-control to move away, storming away in the opposite direction. It would have been a little too easy to delight himself; a few more seconds and he was afraid he wouldn't have been able to stop. She was all that his body longed for, ached for, called out for—but he had to make her see that.

'What...where are you going?' Nandini asked, her voice breathless.

Shivendra did not turn to face her. 'Nowhere you are not coming!' he said, the corner of his mouth twitching. 'I was proving a point and I believe I have succeeded. I am not in the habit of seducing women—when you come to me you will do so because you want to and not because you have been forced to.'

'The only point you have managed to prove by this experiment of yours is the presence of sexual chemistry between us, so why am I better than one of your nautch girls, Shivendra? You don't have to marry me.' Nandini made her point angrily. Was she just a plaything for him, to kiss and then toss aside as fit his little game?

He took a step forward, towering over her, his musky scent all too close. 'We will be married, Nandini. I cannot afford for you to sabotage my reputation, and if you dare refuse, I will ensure your existence is a living hell.'

Refusing to back down, Nandini finally threatened, 'You cannot force me to marry you. I may not be a princess or an heiress but I will not be threatened by you, Yuvraj. I shall pack my bags and return to Multan—my father shall welcome me back with open arms!'

His expression retained its hard lines, but his tone softened. 'The same father who has all his aspirations pinned on his daughter marrying well? Oh yes, I know all that there is to know about you, Nandini.' He saw her expression change instantly, and knew he had touched a raw nerve. 'We will get married, with my parents' blessings, at the family temple once they get back. Since we cannot go back to Jaigarh without creating a scene, we shall journey to Kunihar for my cousin's wedding. If there are any wagging tongues, they will be silenced at the wedding and by the presence of my parents.' Nandini opened her mouth to say something but her voice died within her when she saw the look in Shivendra's eyes.

In spite of herself, she couldn't help getting excited about this—the idea of spending the next few days travelling with Shivendra was extremely enticing. She would enjoy the attraction they shared, and then leave him to marry a more suitable bride; after all, there were nautch girls who enjoyed their conquests, and she too could become one of them, enjoying the pleasures of the flesh.

Her slight pout, the iridescent, endlessly long

eyelashes above large, doe-like eyes, her naivety coupled with the fire that ran through her, her pride, her arrogance—all this invoked in him a feeling so fierce that he wanted to cradle her from the world, to shield her from every danger. He knew the people of Jaigarh would be unforgiving towards her; she didn't stand a chance there. This was the only way out, he had to make her see reason and accept his judgement. The journey to Kunihar would be his last chance, their last chance.

CHAPTER EIGHT

SHIVENDRA WAS NOT PARTICULARLY looking forward to explaining his actions to his mother. Her summons had left the final decision in his hands, for she rarely ordered him around in his personal life, but he had seen the wisdom in her words. He could have compromised Nandini's reputation forever had he gone back to Jaigarh; the people would probably have labelled her wanton, and his father's ministers would have refused to accept his decision to wed her. The only way out of this unholy mess was to get married in Kunihar, in front of his parents, and there would be no better time than this to proclaim his decision. His mother's cousin was getting married in a week's time, and the Rajputs considered it inauspicious to refuse anything during periods of festivities. No doubt it would be difficult for his parents to accept this arrangement but he was sure they would respect his decision and bless their union. As for the people of Kunihar, this marriage would extend their festivities for another month or so—they would be thrilled.

Shivendra had not spoken a word throughout the day, and neither had Nandini; she was waiting for him to say something first. It was an odd sort of truce that they had arrived at. Nandini wondered if he was still cross with her. If he was, she could hardly be blamed. She wasn't used to being bullied like this, and she would never stand for it.

Only, she could feel her heart beat faster as Shivendra casually tightened his hold around the rein of the horse, thus indirectly holding her closer to him. Her heart was pounding so loudly against her ribcage that she was sure he could feel it against his forearm through the thin fabric of her choli. What was the matter with her? Every time Shivendra touched her she felt her body go up in flames; his touch burnt a trail on her porcelain skin.

What was worse was that he looked so unperturbed, so impervious to the contact that was causing her such torment. He could turn it on and off when he wanted—it was apparent. Oh, what would she not give to have such control over one's desires.

They travelled on, riding away from Rajputana, crossing into Punjab from the south-west and then into Himachal, halting only for food and water. Punjab, the food bowl of the nation, was as different from Rajputana as velvety milk was from aged scotch. Rajputana was like an exotic harem dancer, its starkness complemented by the fiery colour of the people's ensembles and temperaments; while Punjab was like a newly married, blushing bride, decked out in all the splendour of a spring morning.

Sunlight beamed down from endless, clear blue skies, polishing the blades of grass with a million dewdrops and giving them a brand new appearance.

The golden of the desert had been replaced by rich hues of green, often offset with the brightest specks of colour in its lovely flowers. Handsome Jat Sikh riders were cantering along the wide pathways, women in vibrant phulkari dupattas were busy churning buttermilk and pounding sesame for the afternoon meal, while their pink-cheeked children munched on succulent fruit, the juice dribbling down their chins.

The Jat Sikhs were a warrior clan, and much like the Rajputs, they were fiercely proud and worthy warriors. Pangs of homesickness shot through Nandini, as she looked around her with longing; the people reminded her of Multan—they dressed similarly, shared a somewhat similar dialect and the same bustle about them that all smaller villages often possessed.

They stopped to share a meal with a farmer's family who knew Shivendra well—a meal of freshly smoked sarson ka saag, makki ki roti doused in butter, and velvety smooth buttermilk that left a layer of ghee in her mouth. Shivendra had often stopped here on his many trips to Kunihar, and the farmer's wife affectionately packed a bag full of ripe fruit for them, newly plucked from their orchard.

They rode on into the evening, crossing the land of the five rivers, the marwar padding with ease on its fertile plains, quenching their thirst at one of the many rivers that flowed across the state. Nandini recalled this was the very place where Lord Buddha had starved and Guru Nanak had wandered in search of the supreme truth. This was the land that had seen many death-defying, eternal love stories like those of

Heer–Ranjha, Sohni–Mahiwal and Mirza–Sahiban. This was the land that had inspired perennial love stories, paramours who had vowed undying passion to each other. Were they destined to follow in their path? Was her fate intertwined with Shivendra's or were they just meant to be strangers, meeting briefly and soon parting ways?

There were so many questions in her mind that only time could answer. She forgot about the past and the future and tried to lose herself in the present. A cool breeze lulled her to sleep as she rested her head on the broad expanse of his chest and closed her eyes.

Nandini awoke when a fat droplet of rain landed on her cheek. She opened her eyes to look around her, calculating they had already bypassed Patiala, after having crossed the Sutlej river, and were a few hours short of Mandi—perhaps between Suket and Mandi. She took in the beauty of the landscape around her. The endless green fields had been replaced by meandering brooks that appeared to be singing to them; pine trees swayed in the wind, as if they were lovers embracing each other after a long separation; while fat droplets pitter-pattered on the already satiated earth; and peacocks danced in all their glory, in perfect sync with the monsoon. The sun had long set, and it would soon be time to halt for the night.

Shivendra calculated the distance to the next village and decided, instead, to stop at one of his maternal grandfather's royal summer retreats. The colossal cottage had been built atop a hill. Vibrant violet blooms marked their path as they made their way upwards. A sliver of a moon gave the landscaped gardens a subtle, diffused glow. Everything was hued with glistening moonlight: the terraces of wheat hovering in the fields, the fragrant apple orchards, the scurrying wild rabbits, and the babbling brooks. Rustic, earthy fragrances swam through the night breeze to them. The two travellers couldn't help but smile.

Above them, a staid and imposing grey structure rose out of the earth, its great stone walls covered with moss, protecting the heart of the kingdom as it had for a thousand years. Shivendra's keen gaze took in the lack of any light in the fort. It would probably be empty, except for a lone housekeeper; the remaining staff would be at Kunihar, celebrating his cousin's nuptials.

His body ached to dismount the horse. Not that he was exhausted; he was well used to riding non-stop for several hours at a stretch, but Nandini was a temptation he was unprepared for. The soaked cotton of her lehenga had moulded itself to her body, accentuating every curve.

He thanked the gods it was already dark and he couldn't ascertain her figure under its flimsy covering. Her firm bottom had been pressed against him for hours, hardening him—with no prospect of release. His forearms had often accidentally grazed the roundness of her breasts, her hardened nipples springing to attention as a result; he felt the rosebuds through the fine layer of muslin, which, ridiculously, was all that separated them. Her touch was electrifying and he involuntarily made a harsh sound at the back of his throat.

'Are you feeling unwell?' Nandini turned around to enquire, moving even closer in the process.

'No. The rain has stopped but it's worth stopping here for the night. I must warn you though, there probably are'nt any servants to do your bidding,' he said.

'I don't need servants, Yuvraj. I am well equipped to take care of myself,' she said.

A young boy came running up to them as they dismounted their horse. 'Yuvraj Shivendra, salaam Huzoor!' He nodded his head a few times before he took the horse's reins. 'The pleasure of your company is completely unexpected, Huzoor, but I will try to arrange everything to your liking.' He bowed to both of them before leading the beast away to the royal stable.

Nandini and Shivendra made their way inside the cottage. Everywhere she looked, Nandini could see the unmistakable evidence of understated wealth; pashmina throws were scattered all around the wooden panels, fluffed-up plush cushions, embossed with the royal seal, were carelessly arranged around an inviting fireplace that heated the chamber. Shivendra led Nandini upstairs to the guest chamber, and without letting his gaze dip below her face, left her there to dry herself.

At Shivendra's suggestion, Nandini rummaged through trunks of priceless shahtooshes and jamewars, that once belonged to the maharani, discarding them all for revealing too much, until she finally decided on a painstakingly hand-embroidered blouse of silk-shahtoosh that wrapped around her body. Even this, however, teasingly hinted at the curves it concealed. Then she put on a loose silk skirt, so fine that it clung to the shape of her legs, outlining the apex of her thighs, which she finally covered with an embroidered piece of silk. She wondered whom these clothes belonged to; they were designed to entice and seduce, to reveal rather than conceal—the type of clothes you wore for a lover in the privacy of your chamber. Selfconsciously, she walked down the polished oak staircase, checking repeatedly to see if her odhna was in place.

Shivendra stood with his back towards her, at the edge of the fireplace, drinking a fiery, amber-coloured liquid. Another swig of the alcohol and he could almost keep Nandini's image from being branded on his mind. Inclining his body against the wooden panel of the fireplace, he sensed her presence, her fragrance already warming his senses.

He turned, and his eyes never reached her eyes, instead lingering on the lushness of her curves; she looked like a goddess sent to answer his silent wish.

A sudden gust of wind swept in through an open window, making the silk cling to her body, and her odhna fluttered away, leaving her body open to his admiring gaze. She grasped frantically in a desperate bid to seize her odhna, but to no avail. Lifted by the breeze, it flew into the air towards the window. Her mane of ebony curls fell loose, and framed her ivory complexion as she lifted her face towards him. Forgetting his earlier resolve, his gaze skimmed the shimmering dress, lingering on the swell of her breasts and her endless legs.

The sound of approaching footsteps provoked him to grab his jamewar throw and hand it to Nandini; she wrapped it around herself swiftly, grateful for something to shield herself from his hot gaze.

'Dinner is served, Huzoor.' It was the servant boy from earlier. 'It is a simple meal, Huzoor, but my mother hopes it will be to your liking. He led them past several connecting chambers until they finally came to the main dining room. The 'simple meal' turned out to be a royal feast, laid out on polished silverware, and consisted of mutton cooked in yogurt and turmeric, fragrant rice deep fried with dry fruits, tandoori rotis stuffed with mince meat, trout cooked in mustard and lemon, fresh fruit with cream, and rice and raisin pudding.

Neither Nandini nor Shivendra could fully enjoy their meal, however, both unsettled by the palpable attraction between them. It seemed as though forever passed before dinner was finished, but forever was actually just half an hour. Nandini retired to her chamber, feigning sleep, and Shivendra drank on.

Today he needed the intoxication more than ever. He tried to centre his feelings on anything and everything except for the woman who now inhabited the suite next to his, but his mind had plans entirely of its own.

Sleep was as obscure as a golden bird, and so he

simply swallowed measure after measure of whisky, until he abandoned his glass and drank straight from the bottle, staring fixedly into the flame of the mashaal that burned a little less fiercely than the fire within him. Every time he gazed into Nandini's eyes, he felt as though he'd somehow always known her, as if they were soulmates from another life. Could the desire that stirred so strongly within him be merely the result of lust or was it something deeper and stronger? Pushing back the sudden vision of Nandini as she had appeared that night, walking down the staircase in practically nothing, he made his way up the twisting staircase, focused on withdrawing to the solitude of his section.

Hearing a noise as he approached her door, he couldn't stop himself; he knew she was alone in there, with no maid or chaperone in her chamber. The sugary scent of rose water overwhelmed his senses, as he stepped inside the room silently.

Nandini was sleeping just as he had imagined her, limbs loose against the bed, loose silk tunic leaving nothing to the imagination. The long hair made a dark cascade from the pillow down to the floor. Her body was bathed in the moonlight streaming in through an arched window, her curls carelessly scattered on her pillow. She moved slightly, mumbling something in her sleep. He moved towards her, compelled by a silent force that he had no control over, until he stood directly in front of her, taking in all her ethereal beauty.

After indulging in the warm bath that had been

laid out for her, Nandini had let an attendant undress her and massage her with a paste of oil and crushed flowers. The light of the moon and stars above came flooding into her room, but Nandini had slept like Kumbhakaran.

But she awoke now, in the middle of the night, sensing the unmistakable presence of someone in the room. She wondered if she had not dreamed it until she saw Shivendra standing at the foot of her bed, clad in white kurta-pyjamas. She shot out of bed with a start, the loose silk falling off her shoulder and exposing one voluptuous breast to his gaze, her nipples immediately so hard that they hurt.

Shivendra stared at her; he had come to check on her as he had heard a loud noise, and finding her sleeping as sweetly as he had imagined, had paused to watch her for a minute. Now, her curves apparent through her tunic, her eyes wild, her breast so tantalizingly laid bare, she looked anything but sweet.

He took a step forward, sweeping her into his arms, easing her on to her still warm bed. He brought his lips to her warm neck as he moved against her, and she moaned in response, her own body moving to match his. He wanted to touch every inch of her body, to taste her sweetness, relish the touch of her nipples on his tongue, to pleasure her until she cried out in ecstasy, begging for more.

Shivendra watched the expression of astonished desire in Nandini's eyes as his mouth took ownership of hers fervently. He kissed her blazing flesh, licking the smouldering skin into a frenzy. Her long legs, spread on either side of his, felt satin smooth under his calloused palms. She was more exhilarating than the alcohol that still surged through his blood, he thought, as he plunged his hands into her hair.

Nandini found herself fastening her arms around his neck, her fingers finding the ties of the kurta and untying the strings, pushing the material from his chest. She could hear the sharp intake of his breath; indeed he was surprised at such a show of passion from his virginal would-be bride. His mouth moved gently against hers, sinking into her velvet warmth while her hands explored, for the first time, what a man's chest felt like—hard, muscled, taut, most pleasantly male.

She pressed her full breasts against his chest, moving against him provocatively, involuntarily, in a movement older than time. Shivendra groaned, removed his lips from hers and traced the line of her neck, her creamy cleavage, with his tongue, planting small kisses in the valley of her breasts. One hand played with a hardened nipple while the other hand slipped around her waist, locking them together in an iron-like grip.

Nandini groaned with pleasure; the fire running through her body was like nothing she had felt before. His arms were hard against her soft body, his unshaven face bristled against her nipples, causing ripples of pleasure.

He bent to suck a tender nipple and then moved on to the other. Nandini's moans of ecstasy were the sweetest sound he had heard.

She tipped his chin forward and kissed his lips—

sweet reward. 'Shivendra,' she moaned, as his finger slipped into her womanhood. Blood pounding, heart racing, she wondered if anything felt this good.

'You *do* want me,' breathed Shivendra, his words hot against her face. She half nodded in acquiescence, driven senseless by his clever, clever hands.

Shivendra tore off her tunic, and then she was bare before him; need flared through him, building up within him like molten lava, till it surpassed anything he had ever known. His hands struggled to undo the string of his pyjamas, but faltered. Nandini stood up, and then, holding his gaze with hers, slipped her fingers where his had been, lowering them, brushing her fingers tantalizingly against him. Shivendra knew this was the point of no return. He wanted her, wanted her with savage desperation. He wanted to feel her beneath him, in the throes of passion, crying out his name in pleasure as he buried himself in her warm softness. He wanted to taste every inch of her porcelain skin, filling her with an intensity that she never knew existed. But was it wise to move this fast? To plunder her before she was his wife?

'Nandini, darling, I won't be able to stop if you continue,' he warned huskily. Nandini ignored him, not wanting to think about where this would lead. But Shivendra knew better. It took all his will power to end their embrace; he didn't want her to regret this decision in the morning. She would come to him willingly, when she was ready, not because he had seduced her in the middle of the night; for this, he realized, was what he had done.

Without another word, he separated her from him, and avoiding the look of utter confusion on her face, walked out of the room. Nandini stared at the receding figure. She wrapped her arms around her bare body, gathered her sheets around her. The room now reflected the gloominess of the clouds outside, circling the moon; it was shrouded in pitch darkness, a darkness that didn't even come close to the dread she felt in her heart. He had seduced her to prove a point, and then, equally brutally, discarded her.

And her feeble attempts to pleasure him? She could see how successful they had been. Men like Shivendra didn't seduce naive virgins like her, they needed the practised touch of Ayesha Begum or a nautch girl. Her heart wept silently as she saw her dreams crumbling. She was in love with a man who felt nothing but pity for her, who would only torture himself by some physical connection that bound them together; one which he might easily find elsewhere, she guessed. After all, what did she know about physical intimacy? She might be mistaking their bond as unique, when obviously it was an ephemeral closeness that all mating couples felt.

She resolved, finally, that this wouldn't stop her from living normally. She would return home, return to her old ways, and be happy in them. She longed to share a laugh with toothless old soldiers describing their experiences at war, to help the village children steal mangoes from the landowners' orchards, and to run around the village and bathe in the lake. She would not let Shivendra take over her life.

CHAPTER NINE

THE NEXT MORNING, NANDINI remembered her decision to start afresh, and pursued her intentions resolutely. She woke to an unexpected optimism, and looked around her. There was not a soul in sight; she decided to explore her surroundings. The serene sanctuary, ensconced between impenetrable cedar forests and imposing snow peaks, was accessible only through trails winding through the fragrant pine forests. Feeling as if she were a part of this fairy tale, Nandini forgot all about the previous night's encounter and looked down at the virgin woods of pine and cedar, from her perch in the Himalayas. This was truly Deva Bhoomi, the Land of the Gods.

Soon she found a clearing, sheltered and private, besides being breathtakingly gorgeous. The river banks were layered in all possible shades of green, while the sun's bright, cheerful rays played hide-and-seek with the emerald trees, and speckled the ground with spots of gold. Nandini stood knee-deep in a carpet of colour—flowers stretched out on either side of her. She lazily sat down and contented herself watching the pretty goldfish bobbing in the water. She dipped her toes into the icy, refreshing water, waiting for the sun to shine brighter before going down to bathe in the brook.

In a week's time she would be back in Jaigarh, and then Multan. She could scarcely wait to see her father again, but a part of her grew heavy at the thought. She shook it off. Shivendra belonged to another world, a world where the likes of her had no place. She was in love with Shivendra, she acknowledged, but she would just have to be satisfied with stolen memories of their relationship, and this would be her cure and consolation. He was more than just an infatuation; during the course of her travels she had discovered a noble, passionate man who was far worthier than the image painted of him in public. He was the love of her life, the man of her dreams, but this was reality—and in real life, princes didn't marry paupers like her. They ended up marrying equally affluent princesses who came with a dowry to match the treasures of Shahenshah Akbar.

She set aside the depressing thought; she couldn't let this dampen her spirits again. There were people who loved her and whom she loved—her happiness was complete with her family, her pet camel Mirchi, her dogs. She would return to her birthplace, back to the dusty bylanes of Multan and to her beloved father. He had written in his last letter that he had managed to pay off most of his loans and was now opening their Lahore haveli to the public, making it an inn of sorts. She would help him run the place, he was much too old. Shivendra had actually done her a favour—now nobody would worry her with proposals of marriage, leaving her to live her life as independently as she pleased.

Satisfied that the water was warm enough, she slipped off her choli and lehenga before she stepped into the stream. She massaged a fragrant crush of herbs and flowers through her long, dark tresses. Then, curving her back, she stepped up, baring her breasts to the chilly air, dipping again into the icy water like a mermaid frolicking in the ocean. Then, she pushed her dishevelled tresses behind her as she bathed her body.

She felt him before she saw him.

He stood behind her, facing the brook, taking in the view, which, in this case, included her. Nandini felt a thrill of excitement in the hollow of her stomach. He was dressed in his riding gear, his scarlet turban with its gold-embossed gota immaculate, his white angrakha spotless, his knee-high weathered leather boots worn over the pyjamas encasing his muscular legs, his sheathed sword gleaming at his side. He looked broad and solid, powerful and menacing. His face gave nothing away; his expression was as blank as an empty canvas, its dimness heightened by his forbidding appearance.

She was horribly aware of her own state of undress. The mountains, the valleys, the orchards and flowers, her new resolve, were all forgotten.

Shivendra was watching her closely, noting her skin as it glistened with droplets of water. Her body looked celestial, like it was decorated with a million gleaming stars, as if she were a goddess descended from the skies. Shivendra could not remove his eyes from the vision that held him captive; the gentle radiance of the partially clouded sun shimmering over her nakedness.

The sight of Nandini's glistening body brought back images from the previous night, rendering him helpless to do anything but watch, entranced by the scene being played out before him. She stepped out from the lake, with nothing more than what nature intended her to wear, still holding his gaze with her own.

Shivendra's breath caught in his throat as she walked towards him, all cream and curves. She halted suddenly, only a few paces from him. Nandini had not intended to flaunt her naked body in front of the yuvraj, especially after last night's humiliation, but her body had a mind of its own. She told herself that she only wanted to check if he was attracted to her, but her heart knew otherwise. Her gaze did not shift, still holding his captive. Her breathing was heavy, her bosom heaving; then, with a haughty lift of her chin, she stood on tiptoe and kissed his lips briefly, pressing her naked, wet body against his, imprinting herself on him. Two could play at this game.

He stared at her for a lingering moment, before turning around and walking uphill to where his horse was tied. The thorny branches slashed and shredded wrathfully at his clothes as he moved through the forest, but Shivendra didn't notice. He stomped uphill in frustration, his face still a mask of some undeterminable expression, his fingers curled into tight balls of exasperation. She was playing with him, and tempting him sorely. But when she came to him, it would be because she was in love with him and not because she mistook lust to be love. He prayed he would be able to wait till then.

Nandini stared at the retreating figure in confusion. She knew he wasn't in love with her, but now he wasn't even attracted to her. Why had she thrown herself at him after the way he behaved with her last night? If she had felt absolute mortification before, she now yearned for the earth to open up and swallow her whole. She would just have to accept that Shivendra would never love her. She rushed towards her discarded skirts and quickly put them on, wetting her garments in the process. She followed him, hurrying, and after a brisk walk, was back at the house. Passing the stables, she noticed five instead of six horses but she thought nothing of it as she barged into the entrance of the cottage via the cobbled pathway, with all the elegance of a sandstorm.

She threw open the doors, hoping it wouldn't be too late, glowing with sweat and out of breath, her unkempt, tousled tresses spreading out behind her.

Like smoke from a hookah, Nandini heard a male voice float towards her—but not the one she hoped to hear, the one that had grown so familiar to her. She turned around to see a sinister-looking man leering at her.

Suddenly she realized her garments were clinging to her wet body. Barely breathing, she watched four rough-looking men approach closer to her. One look and Nandini decided these men were no good, probably outlaws or thieves. Their tattered outfits and filthy appearance proclaimed them to be unquestionably of the very lowest classes. They wore thick, unrefined woollen kurtas and pyjamas, their hands and faces grimy with dirt. Each man carried some sort of weapon, a crudely made dagger or a clumsily fashioned axe in his hand. The biggest man, who was standing in front, appeared to be the most menacing—he had a lecherous expression on his face as he looked at her fixedly, an evil grin at the corner of his mouth.

'I told you this place would be inhabited by apsaras,' he told the others. The other two men, both with equally crude looks on their faces, joined in the laughter that reverberated through the hall.

'What beauty! When it rains, it surely does pour!' the tall man announced in a harsh, lascivious voice as he came to a halt, staring at her. 'Surely this angel has been sent to us to satiate us, what creamy skin!' he said to the biggest of the filthy men. 'I wonder if she tastes as sweet as she looks.'

'The only thing you will be able to taste will be your toothless gums, after this incident,' a voice announced from the parted doors. Shivendra walked into the open courtyard with cool insolence, his hand resting lightly on his sword. 'Step back, Nandini, and cover yourself,' he commanded, throwing his pashmina shawl to her.

'It is Yuvraj Shivendra,' the third man whispered in reverence. The name was evidently self-explanatory as the men all took a step back.

But the leader of the group raised his eyebrow and surveyed the yuvraj with a half-mocking smile. 'The prince himself; what an honour to kill a yuvraj!' he said with a flourish. His companions cowered behind him, looking at their leader as if he were mad. 'Come now, you cowards—a yuvraj without his army is not a real yuvraj, he's just an ordinary man,' he urged them fiercely.

Nandini watched in panic as the men surrounded Shivendra.

'We shall see!' Shivendra drew out his sword and positioned himself to fight. The men attacked him remorselessly, aiming blows at his waist, neck, and shoulders, and the prince continued to avoid each one, sending the men reeling as he sparred and parried.

He could feel the blood streaming down his nose from a few cuts. He knew that these men were dangerous, and that if anything were to happen to him, they would not spare Nandini. He signalled for her to leave, but Nandini only came closer, looking desperately for a sword of her own, so she could step into the fray.

'It is time to give them a taste of their own medicine,' Shivendra thought. He swiftly and expertly raised his left leg and brought down the men surrounding him. Then, taking advantage of the confusion of the two who assailed him, he dealt them several blows, knocking them down.

'Watch out!' Nandini warned as one of the assailants tried to strike him again.

Shivendra turned casually, and quick as lightning,

struck him hard in the gut. The attackers fell down in a pile of bodies, all over each other, and remained there, fearful of more punches and kicks.

'Remove yourselves from my premises right now,' Shivendra thundered at the men. The bloodied men picked themselves up and made off, limping. Just then, the servant boy came running up, a few men behind him—Nandini had run to get him to call for help, as Shivendra fought on. The village folk led the men away; the king would deal with them later.

Nandini, the unwitting centre of this fracas, came running towards Shivendra and checked the extent of his injuries. She quickly tore off an edge of her odhna and wound it across his bleeding abdomen; he had suffered one large cut. Without thinking, she embraced him. They stood like that for a while, feeling the warmth of each other's breath and bodies.

'Shivendra, you're bleeding,' Nandini said, tears pooling in her eyes. Shivendra placed his hands on either side of her face and kissed her forehead lightly. 'Forget all about it, collect your things—we should get moving.'

'But what about your wound? You are bleeding, we can't carry on like this,' she protested, her fingers brushing against the fresh wound.

'I feel well enough to ride; this is a minor cut, don't look so worried,' he said, holding her face tenderly. 'Now go, collect your things.'

Shivendra could feel himself losing his strength—the fight had weakened him more than he cared to confess. But it wasn't safe to linger here in an unprotected cottage—the men might have more outlaw friends who would come to look for them.

The two readied their things and rode off, passing through neighbouring towns. The local folk stared; there was something about Nandini—beauty and grace, and some indefinable air of femininity about her—that proclaimed that she was a woman of noble birth, despite her soiled clothes. The yuvraj was recognizable to the locals as well, and they stared at his dishevelled appearance—his cream angrakha was ripped and stained with blood at various places. The jamewar hid his bleeding torso, but it was just a matter of time before he would need medical help.

It was already approaching nightfall, and tomorrow they would reach Kunihar. He stopped outside a cottage plastered with cow dung, then, jumping off the horse, he wrapped a shawl around his face and knocked softly on the wooden door at the entrance. It would be best to keep his identity a secret. The door was opened by a middle-aged man with kind eyes and a prematurely grey beard. He surveyed the couple standing in front of him.

'Huzoor, we need a place to spend the night.' Shivendra bowed to the man with respect.

'Of course, my son! You are our guests and all guests are like God. Bring your horse in as well—he can feed on the grass growing in my yard,' the man said, ushering both of them inside. 'Wash up at the well behind the house, we were just sitting down for dinner,' he said, leading them towards the well. Shivendra and Nandini dutifully washed their hands and faces before joining the man and his wife for dinner, playing the part of a soldier home from the army; one who had been involved in a skirmish. They partook of steamed millet bread and mutton cooked in lentils, humble yet tasty fare.

'Such a handsome couple you two make! How long have you been married?' the man's wife asked. Nandini blushed, and Shivendra accepted the compliment evenly. 'Oh, don't be shy,' the lady of the house said, scooping sweet rice, liberally mixed with raisins and dry fruit, from the copper pot and piling it on Shivendra's and Nandini's plates. 'Here, try this with some ankalo cakes.'

After the meal, Shivendra and Nandini were shown into a room. 'I hope this will do, it is our son's room. It opens out to a private bathing area at the back,' said their hostess, opening the creaky back door. 'If you need anything, you can call me.'

The two were left alone. Shivendra groaned as he checked his wound, and Nandini silently bent down near his side. Her fingers moved around the bloody, disfiguring marks of the wounds on his left side, soothing, healing.

His naked chest heaved in what she could only imagine as pain. The muscles of his exercised and honed body flexed involuntarily. Even wounded, the sheer maleness of his body took her breath away.

Shivendra lay back on a divan as Nandini traced his wound with her delicate fingers. She turned away for a brief second, wetting the muslin in a pitcher of cold water, then, expertly placing a film of crushed moss green herbs on the cut. She soothed it with the rag in her hand. After repeating the process, she moved away from him to cut her odhna up further so she could bandage him with it. Shivendra appeared to have fallen asleep, a steady, calm breathing emanating from his chest. His feet dangled on one side of the bed, and his eyes were firmly shut. Glancing down at his bloodstained torso, she sat at the edge of the bed, placing a cold hand on his forehead. 'I am sorry, this was all because of me,' she whispered, barely loud enough for him to hear.

As she bent over him, Shivendra suddenly opened his eyes. He tugged her hand slightly, fitting it into his palm. As he lifted himself with one arm, he turned to face her directly, took her by the elbow, and laid her on his chest, her back to the ceiling. 'I might hurt you, Shivendra,' she whispered.

'Shhh, I will be fine.' He kissed her eyes, then the tip of her nose. Her back thrilled at his touch.

Shivendra's lips touched hers in the softest kiss yet—gentle and soft, yet deeply passionate. Exploring her, teasing her. She felt the same invigorating rush of emotions that hit her every time he kissed her, or touched her, or even looked at her; she felt like she had never been kissed before. Intuitively, she parted her lips, welcoming the invasion of his tongue into her mouth. Shivendra groaned; she had learnt fast, and well. Gathering her pliant body to his, he escalated the intensity of their kiss, teasing her and nipping her lips, drawing away when she demanded more and plunging into her sweetness when she least expected it.

This kiss was fiery, hot-blooded, zealous; it was everything she imagined it would be and more. Every rational thought was erased from her memory; she could now understand what women meant when they complained of a man stealing their sleep. In this case, Shivendra had stolen her breath; she had forgotten what it was like to breathe, to live, to be without him.

Shivendra pulled her as close as it was humanly possible to, moulding her body to his, feeling every curve, every inch of her body with his hands, while he kissed her again with passion, assaulting her hot, wet lips with his tongue.

There was a sudden knock on the door and he straightened up and disengaged himself from her. Nandini opened the door—it was their hostess. 'I brought you this,' she said, bringing in some well-worn but immaculately clean clothes. She glanced briefly at Shivendra's exposed shoulders—he had draped the shawl to cover his wound—and smiled knowingly at Nandini. 'Now don't let me disturb you two.'

Nandini moved away, embarrassed. The man was wounded and she couldn't keep her hands off him.

Shivendra grinned, then began to prepare for bed, exhausted from the day's fighting yet exhilarated, now. The two prepared to sleep, moving away to opposite ends of the large bed in the centre of the room.

Nandini couldn't sleep, so she got out of bed and walked over to the window. She watched Shivendra's steely torso glisten under the moonlight as he flung his shawl away, a lump forming in her throat as desire overcame her. She was a clay doll in his hands, one that he could craft and mould according to his whims and fancies. But deep inside her, she craved to be regarded as more than just an object of desire; just as she saw him as more than that. She didn't want Shivendra to marry her out of lust or duty, but love.

'Shivendra,' Nandini hesitated. She desperately sought reassurance; she needed to know if his future actively included her, or if she was just another amusing diversion.

'Hmmm?' he asked, stripping her with his eyes. Her courage deserted her then, and she turned her back on him, shrugging the question away. He watched the tension in her back and rose to join her near the window. They stood beside each other in companionable silence for a while, watching the starry skies and the majestic, white-topped mountains in the distance. Shivendra slipped a hand into hers, lowering his face to graze the side of her neck.

'What is it that makes you frown, jaan?' he asked, his eyes softening with concern.

'I...I am just scared. I am very scared of tomorrow, Shivendra,' she whispered, so quietly that if it weren't for the still of the night, her voice would have disappeared without reaching his ears.

'Scared?' he questioned, turning her sideways to face him. 'You have no reason to be scared, Nandini. I will always be there at your side, through pain and sickness, through conflicts and worries.'

A tear rolled down her cheek and he reached out

to wipe it away. 'Shhh, what are you scared of, my dearest? Tell me,' he half asked, half commanded. 'Did I offend you in any way?'

'No, no, just...just...' It was her turn to reach out to him now. She traced her delicate fingers over the contours of his face—which were so fascinating to her—brushing over his stubble and moving down to his neck.

A ragged groan escaped his throat as he clasped her fingers to kiss their tips. 'What is it, Nandini? Is my love not enough?' he breathed roughly.

'L...love? Did you say love?' she asked disbelievingly, her hands still.

'Of course I said love. You know I love you like I have never loved anyone before.'

'But you said you were marrying me to save my honour, my reputation, and...' she babbled, her cheeks flushing with excitement.

'Only so you would agree to come with me, my love. I wanted, no...needed this time to make you believe how much I loved you. More than my life, Nandini. More than anything in this world.'

He looked at her with such gentleness, she felt she had come home, after a long time. 'Oh Shivendra, what a fool I've been!' She eased herself into his arms, her hands linking behind his shoulders. 'All this time I thought you were just...playing with me.'

'Now, that's not a bad proposition, is it?' he teased. 'I could spend an eternity ravishing you,' he murmered, cradling her closer into his arms and there they stood, bathed in moonlight for what seemed like eternity.

The next morning, having thanked their hosts profusely, the couple rode off towards Kunihar. They passed marketplaces selling the ordinary and the exotic; pink-faced children chasing wild pigs through narrow alleys; winding pathways leading to nowhere in particular; and charming wooden cottages with creeper-covered walls. They finally approached the nerve centre of Kunihar. Despite the untimely hour and the nip in the air, the markets of Kunihar were swarming with people. Hawkers attempted to sell their merchandise to locals preparing for the day. Horsemen trotted down cobbled pathways, not bothering to award the pedestrians anything more than a glance. Plump, shiny-faced children, wearing woollens that weighed more than they did, darted about the market place, pulling each others' hair and sticking out their tongues at strangers. The streets were lined with succulent fruit freshly picked from the orchards, and fragrant flowers that were being strung into gajras.

Glittering glass bangles from Ferozabad; lengths of chiffon, painstakingly embroidered with silver wire brought all the way from Hyderabad; elaborately engraved silver jewellery boxes from Jaipur; uncut diamond earrings from the south of Gujarat; and the softest imaginable shahtoosh wraps from Afghanistan greeted their sight as they made their way through the market. The bazaar was decked out in all the splendour of a bright sunny morning. Nandini watched in rapt fascination as vendors displayed and customers bargained. Shivendra, however, was miles away.

He knew it was time to take charge of his life and his estate, and the responsibilities that went with his rank. It was time, in other words, to grow up and be the man he was expected to be, by his father, his people, and even himself. Shivendra gazed up towards the palace that would be his inheritance and realized he would have a lot of explaining to do for his rash actions of late.

Cantering faster, he rode into the main gate of the palace, acknowledging the guards' salutation with a brief nod of his head. The scene that greeted them was of chaotic festivity.

Mehendi was being applied to women's hands, shehnais were being played against the rhythm of a variety of musical instruments. The couple descended the blue-carpeted staircase and entered the main hall. Shivendra took Nandini's hand in his and stood there, rooted to the spot.

The mass of people in the room froze, immobile for a minute. A bewildered pause replaced the incessant chatting and gossip. It seemed to Nandini as though everyone had turned into statues in a split second, expressions of horror on their faces. Then, just as abruptly, the expressions of shock were replaced by fake smiles and people resumed their activities.

The guests gossiped in hushed whispers, wondering about Nandini's identity, just loud enough for the couple to overhear.

'Has Shivendra taken a bride, finally?' a woman in a lace outfit asked, peering at her companion's sour expression.

A few yards away, a young woman, decked in all the colours of Holi, burst into tears. 'Not fair—I wanted to marry him, Ma hukum; you promised I would be his bride!' she howled.

Everyone wanted to know who this woman was. Nandini knew this scene would turn into a scandal, spawning gossip for days to come over tea and over dinner parties. But she and Shivendra were past caring.

Shivendra ignored the crush and strode towards the main hall, the crowds automatically making way for him. Nandini matched his steps as they passed the lined guests, the astonished servants, and the chattering mothers. They walked past rows of smiling old grandparents—who were straining to catch a glimpse of the handsome couple—before stepping into a crowd of people gathered in the heart of the room, under the chamber's wide dome adorned with chandeliers.

Shivendra kept her close by his side. Nandini grasped his arm and looked at the floor for fear she would trip, occasionally raising her eyes to smile as widely as she could.

They were soon interrupted. The maharani, Shivendra's mother, stepped in their way, stalling their steps. She took her son by the hand and drew him aside, murmuring a few words into his ears. Words Nandini wasn't able to hear. A few minutes of muttered conversation later, Shivendra came towards her, and supporting her back with his palm, drew her towards the quiet privacy of a nearby chamber, turning to inform both his mother and her that he had decided to wed Nandini in Kunihar.

His mother gasped dramatically, but quickly covered her shock and hugged Nandini awkwardly. 'Yes, yes, that will be the best way to quieten rumours. Now my child, I must prepare you to look like a bride, come with me,' she said, leading Nandini towards a connecting chamber. 'Shivendra, wash yourself and change into something clean,' she said, as a parting note.

Then she closed the door, and Nandini was alone with her.

CHAPTER TEN

NANDINI'S ANIMATED, KOHL-LINED EYES, usually so spirited and luminous with fiery will, had turned fluid with trepidation as she followed the maharani down a maze of corridors lined with blazing torches. Precious silver consoles, piled with trinkets of ruby and emerald, shone like a soldier's newly polished swords. Tiny, resplendent crystals of the chandeliers around them, edged with gold and pregnant with the million candles burning within them, shimmered like a nautch girl's poshaak.

'Now hurry along, you have to be ready before the puja begins.' The Maharani of Jaigarh's voice resonated within the labyrinth of corridors, startling Nandini. The bride-to-be hurried behind the maharani nervously, in an effort to catch up with her, her lehenga swishing around her delicate ankles.

She stared at the outsized, daunting portraits of ancestors long past, facing each other on either side of the walls. The maharani followed Nandini's gaze, and mistaking her anxiety for interest, launched into a brief history of her ancestors.

'Nandini, you know, the man dressed in gold was my great grandfather. He only wore gold—he even insisted on eating food which had a layer of beaten gold encasing it! And that one—the one with a tiger at his feet—was very fond of domesticating wild animals. He had seventeen wild cats, which they released into the forests when they started eating the servants for supper. The lady on the left was my grandfather's mother, and the only woman to have her portrait painted in Kunihar—purdah was so strictly observed that she posed for the portrait in a veil and the painter couldn't make out her features through the chiffon, so he used his imagination to create something entirely different.' She laughed, and Nandini found herself joining in. She had never thought the yuvraj's mother would have been this nice. What had he said to sway her?

'I have asked Shakuntala to arrange a room for you in the zenana, at the rear of the palace, so you will have sufficient privacy,' the maharani said, her voice both gentle and authoritative at the same time. 'If you need anything, you can ring the silver bell in your room—Shakuntala will see to it that you have it.' They walked on, passing the many suites and halls, through open terraces with brass swings and lotus ponds, till they reached an open garden. The fragrance of roses surrounded them, enveloping them in its sweet aroma. A suite of chambers stared at them, bathed by the reflecting glow of the lake around it, one that twinkled with the morning sun's rays.

'These used to be my chambers when I was a girl,' the maharani said softly, reminiscing. 'You know, they have a separate entrance at the back that opens out to the city. I used to steal away on winter mornings, dressed in the garb of a maid, just to know what it felt like to walk into markets unescorted,' she continued with a wicked gleam in her eyes. So the maharani too knew what it felt like to want to stray from the conventional, Nandini thought, surprised, warming to this dignified, understanding woman.

'Nandini,' she said finally, clearing her voice, stopping in her tracks to turn her gaze sideways. 'I was wrong about you—if my son's happiness lies with you, you have my blessings. Whatever you two decide, I will always support you, but do remember that Shivendra is the next Maharaja of Jaigarh and Kunihar, so think carefully of the circumstances.'

Nandini swallowed hard under the maharani's stern eye, a wave of emotions washing over her unexpectedly. She nodded shyly, and lowered her head to fix her eyes on the peridots embedded on the cool marble floor at her feet.

The maharani carried on. 'I have asked my maids to send up some of my silk brocade poshaaks and jewels suitable for the occasion, till I can have some more made to your measurements.' She cleared her throat and looked at Nandini. 'Now, I understand this...position will entail a lot of adjusting at your end, but I expect you to behave like a yuvrani. Do you understand what I mean?'

'Yes, Hukum. I understand and will try my best not to fail you or the kingdom,' Nandini said, hurriedly looking away lest the maharani notice the alarm on her face.

'Good, now I don't want to make a scene in front of everyone, which,' she raised an eyebrow, looking at Nandini with a slight smile at the corner of her mouth, 'no doubt, both of you have already succeeded in creating, so please keep the reason for your appearance a secret until a formal announcement.'

She reached over and rang the bell, answering the look of alarm on Nandini's face before it could be voiced in words. 'You know how people talk!' she told her, brushing Nandini's concern away.

Shakuntala appeared, carrying a plate of almond sweetmeats. The matriarch gave her some very unusual tasks. 'Shakuntala, there you are. Take Nandini to her chamber and dress her up for the evening. Dress her up in the red brocade that I wore for my father's coronation; and my grandmother's diamonds and rubies. I want her to be bathed and massaged with walnut oil and then ensure you do her solah singaar.'

'The diamonds?' Shakuntala asked, in shock, then looking at her mistress's face, she quickly bent her head down. 'Of course, Hukum,' she stammered, looking at Nandini incredulously as her mistress walked away. Shakuntala took a suspicious look at Nandini's ripped and stained cotton lehenga. What was this strangeness, the maid wondered, as she led the bride-to-be to her chamber.

Nandini followed her and began to ready herself. Stepping out for a minute to look for Shakuntala, who had gone to fetch hot water, she was distracted by a tall tumbler of refreshing sherbet, at the far end of the corridor. She suddenly felt very thirsty and decided to get a glass of the cooling drink before retiring to her chamber again. Nobody paid her any attention as she walked the length of the hallway silently, and she found herself outside a slightly ajar oak door.

The voices within were loud enough for her to hear.

'Conniving, I tell you...to hook Shivendra...'

'Oh these women from lower-middle-class homes stop at nothing, even throwing themselves and seducing...Nandini, isn't it?'

Nandini stood just outside the room, willing herself to turn away, but it was as if her feet were stuck in coal tar, held in place by an unseen force. Slowly, she looked through the peephole.

A lady in a rich peacock-blue tissue lehenga was reaching out for an enormous laddoo, while chomping on something she had already stuffed in her mouth. She rattled on, obviously enjoying the attention. 'He won't marry a woman without station. This is just a big drama. And his mother is simply going along with this charade.'

Another woman, dripping with jewels, peered at her unconvincingly. 'You understand this is a very delicate matter for that girl, don't you? I have heard the maharani has decided to take full responsibility of her wedding; she told the girl's aunt that she will give her a dowry that Jaigarh will remember for ages, but we can't be sure of anything till things go back to normal.'

'Oh, please. You women worry too much. My cousin's daughter-in-law's aunt overheard the maharani tell her maid that she was only playacting. They will go back to Jaigarh and announce to the kingdom that they were all travelling together; and as for that unfortunate episode about the abduction, how long will people talk? Sooner or later, they will forget about the episode and find something more entertaining.'

Nandini stood there in shocked silence, watching the episode take place as a third lady, whom she recognized as Shivendra's aunt, joined in. 'There is no chance that a gold-digger like that girl will be the next yuvrani.'

Nandini gasped involuntarily at the insult, and the door moved open under her hands. All the women turned to stare at her. Shivendra's own family, her family-to-be, thought she had plotted this.

She could hardly hear what the women were saying now—the room was closing in on her, and her heart was pounding so loudly in her ears and filling her throat that it was difficult to even breathe. A whore? A gold-digger? Surely they weren't talking about her. Tears suddenly blinded her, and Nandini, beginning to panic, looked around for an exit.

She walked out of the room in a trance. Shivendra was not planning to marry her—all his promises, his dedication, everything was a big lie. If his family was saying it, it had come from him, she was sure. She felt her head pound as if a million axes were hacking it, and hastily slipped out into the night, running down the corridors and out of a back entrance.

She didn't want Shivendra to marry her out of sympathy; she had hoped he would have fallen in love with her, but she had been wrong. How could she have forgotten that humiliating night of rejection when he had walked away from her, leaving her frustrated and unfulfilled? If she wanted to act, it would have to be now.

An explosion of cold, frosty air hit her already shivering body, and she pulled the cotton odhna tighter around herself. Nandini shivered in the bitterly cold air as she made her way down to the town, but she did not turn back to the palace behind her, in spite of the tempting warmth of the burning torches shining from their brackets in the wall. She walked on into the unknown, past the kitchen garden and the royal stables. She forced her protesting body to continue its descent, finally reaching the beginnings of a rambling marketplace, despite an inner voice warning her to turn back. She spotted a carriage stand at the mouth of the market and walked purposefully towards it.

'I want a carriage to go to Jaigarh,' she said bravely to the man standing nearby one. He looked at her incredulously. 'All the way to Jaigarh? You will have to change carriages twice and it will cost you two silver pieces,' he said gruffly, looking at her appearance.

'Two pieces? I don't have two pieces of silver but I can give you this.' She removed her diamond solitaire earrings. 'They were my mother's and cost much more than two pieces of silver.'

The man stared at her greedily. 'All right, sit there,' he said excitedly, grabbing the earrings and pointing towards a stone ledge on the other side. 'I will have to speak with my partner.' Nandini wrapped the cotton odhna around herself even tighter and perched herself on the ledge, waiting.

An image of the gaily dressed women at the wedding came into her mind suddenly and she realized that as the daughter of an impoverished zamindar she would never be considered worthy enough to occupy the position of a yuvrani, in these sophisticated, genteel circles. She would always be considered an outcast by the princely states. Shivendra would be better off marrying a princess of his own stature, who wouldn't be judged by her virtues but by the size of her dowry, her status and station.

'You! Your carriage is departing,' the carriage driver screamed out to her, breaking into her thoughts. Nandini stepped inside the coach and closed the door behind her.

The door was suddenly pulled open again, letting in a gush of bitter air. Not bothering to turn her face away from the window, Nandini looked on outside. A shadow came over her face; she could sense the warmth of another person in the narrow confines of the carriage. A feeling of alarm gripped her. She turned her head slowly, raised her eyebrows in defiance, before her eyes locked with Shivendra's all-too-familiar eyes.

Panic ate at her. 'You forgot your earrings,' he said, with an expression that gave nothing away, opening his fist to reveal her solitaire earrings. Nandini was too baffled to speak.

He looked imposing, imperious, every inch the next Maharaja of Jaigarh and Kunihar. He had evidently bathed and changed, the open-necked ivory coat perfectly fitting his powerful body. Now, he took the seat opposite her, warming his hands by rubbing them together.

For a bare moment, Nandini just stared at his profile. 'So where are we going now? Looks like you haven't had your fill of adventures.' He gave her a lazy smile that turned her insides into mush.

'Shivendra, how did you find me?' she asked quietly, willing herself not to fly into his arms.

'I have my sources.' He looked at her quivering lower lip; then ran his eyes over her face. He suddenly turned serious and formidable. 'Why are you leaving?' he asked, looking straight at her.

Why are you leaving? Not why are you leaving me? She was entirely susceptible to his charm. Nandini eased back into her seat, heart galloping faster than wild horses, as he raised a hand to her quivering lower lip.

'You are not in love with me, at least not the right way, that's why. And they will never accept us for what we are, even your own aunts know what you think of me!' she blurted, her face flushed. The tears that she had bottled up within her rose to the surface. Shivendra looked down affectionately at her tear-stained face. He took her face in his hands and kissed the tip of her nose. 'You are the love of my life, Nandini,' he said intensely, pleading her to believe. 'Ask me how difficult it was to walk away from you all those times, my darling, but I wanted time to make you fall in love with me.'

The sun was lowering now; it was not quite dusk, but nearly. As she stepped outside, the light grew soft all around her, throwing purple shadows across the grass and trees.

She looked at him, still not knowing whether to put her faith in his words. 'I thought I had lost you forever, my love', he said, and her heart lurched and gave a little flip. 'I want to marry you, I want you to be the mother of my children, and I want to grow old with you,' he said tenderly, as his hand brushed back a wayward lock of glossy hair from her forehead.

Nandini was too struck by the ensuing wave of emotions to say anything; the endless stream of tears flowing down her porcelain cheeks were answer enough. 'And your family? All those people who...who think I am not worthy of you?' she sobbed.

'I don't care about them. My mother adores you, my father is happy I have decided to settle down. As for the rest, let barking dogs bark. Remember, these are the same people who thought me incapable of ruling Jaigarh; the same voices have called me irresponsible and labelled me a Casanova, yet they never tire of trying to fix me up with their daughters. Ignore them; you are my life, my love, and that's all that matters,' Shivendra said, as he raised one finger to wipe Nandini's tears away.

In the dimly lit carriage, Shivendra brought her hand up to his mouth and kissed it tenderly. Then he moved towards her, imprisoning her yielding body between the carriage wall and the hard contours of his own frame. Her eyes widened as he bent his head to cover her mouth with his, plunging into her warm mouth with a hungry kiss. 'Let's go home,' he breathed, his voice husky with desire. It was a statement, not a question or a suggestion. 'Or...'

His mouth curved into a lopsided smile. 'Or we could just stay here,' he teased, his face breaking into a warm smile.

She smiled and looked up into his burning eyes, shaking her head. When she kissed him again, it was after her own whispered confession of love.

They sat there, hand in hand, lost in each other's eyes, till a meek voice interrupted them. 'The...carriage is supposed to leave now, Huzoor. Except...if you want it to stay, of course.' It was the carriage driver, all folded hands and lowered eyes now.

The prince shook his head, and the couple descended, approaching the yuvraj's horse. After he had hoisted them both on to the horse's back, he grasped the reins of the beast, then jabbed his jootis firmly into its sides. The horse reared, and then leapt forward.

They raced along the cobbled road, the chill of the evening air piercing their skin and stinging their eyes, Shivendra turned Nandini's face towards his chest. She breathed in his familiar musky smell, resting her face against the protection of his broad shoulders. He sighed, and hugged her closer. All that was important to him was close to him.

CHAPTER ELEVEN

THE MAHARANI, WITH TEARS in her eyes, welcomed them with burning lamps and an enormous plate laden with auspicious kumkum, turmeric and curd. 'You are like my daughter; yes, I was mistaken about you earlier, but I knew you were the one for my son the second I laid eyes on you.' The women of the palace had explained everything, telling of the scene Shivendra's aunt had created with her malicious gossip.

The maharani wept, hugging Nandini tightly before giving a curt nod to the women in waiting—all of whom had their heads hung down in shame—scorching them with her stare, before sweeping out of the room.

The entire town soon gathered at the palace to celebrate the wedding of Yuvraj Shivendra to his Nandini. After two weeks of endless festivities, the ceremony culminated in a grand wedding. Endless tables laden with delicacies cooked by the Jaigarh cooks were being sampled by the Kunihar nobility: delicious, spicy lal maas, tender, doughy naan, daal smothered in butter, partridge left to bake overnight in the womb of the earth, the creamy meat fresh from shikaar, and a spread of sumptuous desserts prepared from khoya and jaggery.

In the meantime, Shakuntala had bathed and dressed Nandini for the evening of festivities stretching in front of them. A paste of oil, turmeric, and gram flower was used to cream and scrub Nandini's hands and arms. Following a warm bath with milk and rose water, she was draped in a lehenga of the softest silk brocade, woven in pure gold thread. The choli was a heavy gold-and-red silk, with tassels fastening the skimpy garment to her back. A heavier tissue odhna veiled her face from the public, but made it easy for her to observe her surroundings without being watched. The maids scrupulously threaded tiny pink pearls and sparkling precious stones into her tightly-braided hip-length hair.

Nandini stood on the terrace outside her room, watching the rays of the sun dance on the sapphire lake overlooking her suite. She was getting married today. She sat down next to the marble pond in the centre of the terrace; glancing down at her reflection in the still waters, she saw a beaming face staring back at her. She could not tell if she looked pretty but she knew she looked blissfully happy. This was the most celebrated day of her life. Today, she would marry the man she had secretly loved since the day she had seen him. She dipped a finger into the icy water to make sure this wasn't a dream.

'Hukum, it is time, are you ready?' a young maid came for her, bending over and lifting Nandini's heavy lehenga around the ankles so she could walk.

As she walked towards the ceremony hall, the women behaved as differently as shining silver was to tin. They hovered around Nandini and praised her poshaak, the way she spoke, the way she looked. She ignored their efforts, instead concentrating on the banjara dancers dancing expertly to the steady rhythms of the drum, lanterns balanced effortlessly on their heads and hands.

Everything seemed different. Her eyes searched for the one man who was her entire existence but couldn't locate him.

Shadows chiselled his jagged outline as he observed the swarming foyer from the dimly lit, towering veranda; in the vacillating flame of the wall mounted mashaal, Shivendra seemed to glimmer in and out of the scene like a voiceless spectre—proud and elegant. The blazing fire glimmered over his midnight-black hair and caught the glint of happiness in his eyes. Today he would marry the woman he loved, breaking tradition and convention. All that mattered was how much he loved her. With a thoughtful expression, Shivendra lifted the stone-encrusted crystal goblet of claret wine to his lips, pausing to inhale its mellow bouquet before he drank.

Alcohol and good wishes flowed in equal plenty at the hall below him. A few women were escorting Nandini down the stairs to the main hall. His Nandini.

She looked like a rose in full bloom, as she blushed at a comment made by the lady on her left. Then, lifting her eyes she searched the room for, he hoped, himself. Not having spotted him, she moved through the crowd like a swan across a lake, all grace and slender beauty. Her skin was the palest white, making a sharp contrast to her ink-black hair, though the gentle rose of good health graced her cheeks. His eyes caressed her face, resting on her intoxicating eyes, before moving down to her sweetly curved body. They had met in just such circumstances, in just such a room—but this time, it was different. They now knew each other, each other's perfections and imperfections.

The high colour in her cheeks, the quick rise and fall of her bosom, the way her fingers clutched the heavy material of her pink lehenga—Shivendra couldn't take his eyes away from the vision that greeted him, bound him in a spell so strong that he was in jeopardy of being bewitched by this goddess all his life. Not that he minded.

Everything about her, from her infectious laughter to her dreamy, sparkling eyes displaying steely determination, from her fearless energy to the breeding that gave her such poise and dignity, everything set her apart from all other women. The air was heavy with the whiff of intoxicating perfume. Guests in vivid colours spoke in whispers as Shivendra walked down to join his young bride, her face instantly lighting up like a hundred diyas.

The couple locked their gaze amidst the sound of the shehnai and drums drifting up to the twinkling skies of Kunihar. A great fire threw an orange and red glow about the room, and Nandini's long sable curls reflected the hues of the fire, as the rites were performed. From afar, she glimpsed her ecstatic aunt Shreyas, and in another corner, Devika and Manvendra—who, Shivendra informed her, following Manvendra's proposal, were now engaged. The search for Nandini had brought Devika closer to the man she had earlier found so infuriating, and the two were to be married next month. They all waved at her happily.

As she walked around the sacred fire, Nandini smiled as Shivendra looked back at her lovingly; the future was theirs.

EPILOGUE

THE MOONLIT SILVER SANDS glittered before Nandini's eyes, against a background of craggy mountains. Her wedding to Shivendra, their reception in Jaigarh, her teary reunion with her father, everything seemed an eternity away. Some memories were clear; others felt like the fragments of a dream. Nandini looked around her, at the sandstone haveli, which had been especially built by her besotted groom as a wedding present for her. It had been assiduously hand-polished to resemble Surya the sun god's chariot. The beautiful haveli housed an eclectic range of prized paintings and sculptures; life-sized marble busts bought from the Portuguese in exchange for their weight in silver; Spanish porcelain tiles; and exquisitely woven Persian carpets.

Against the background of the palace that she inhabited with her husband, the tall palm trees that surrounded the property shone. There was a sweet scent of desert flowers in the air, the recent rain having brought them back to life. Nandini stared at the calm of the desert beyond, Shivendra's arm lightly resting around her waist. His eyes were full of love and adoration for his new bride.

They had found love in the desert, Nandini remembered, and now they would continue to have this love.

'Happy, my love?' asked the yuvraj.

'Only as happy as you are,' replied Nandini. She added mischievously, 'Or you'll take a mistress. I know how fond you are of those!'

Shivendra laughed. He could never tire of Nandini's wit, her playfulness, the fire that had drawn him to her. 'You're forgetting, Yuvrani, that I married my mistress.'

Nandini laughed, nodding. 'I'm glad you did,' she whispered, as he drew her close.

A NOTE ON THE AUTHOR

Sanyogita Rathore read her first romance novel at the impressionable age of thirteen in boarding school and has been hooked ever since. The next five years saw her breaking every rule in boarding school, from bunking classes and reading romance under the bed, to hiding in her cupboard with a tiny torch to guide her through the magical story, while the matron forced the others to eat inedible dinner.

OTHER TITLES IN THE SERIES

GHAZAL IN THE MOONLIGHT
Alessandra Shahbaz

Dazzling Shameena runs wild in the Nawab's palace in Lucknow until her weak-willed father promises her to Nicholas Winthrop, the richest Englishman in the subcontinent. Furious about the alliance, she rebels and flees her father's home, disguised as a courtesan. But when Asef, the thrillingly mysterious bodyguard of Nicholas, is dispatched to bring her back, Shameena finds herself caught in a dangerous game, between East and West, fire and ice...

THE ZAMINDAR'S FORBIDDEN LOVE
Jasmine Saigal

Madhubati, the beautiful, feisty daughter of a Bengali teacher who tutors sons of rich zamindars, is pledged to Bidyut, the son of a family friend. But when fate brings her father's dashing student Som into her life, just as it did six years ago, the voluptuous village belle is forced to choose between fighting against their families—and against her fast-beating heart. Will love prevail over reason and class?